D0396692

Alia Waking

Alia Waking

23270

46175

Laura Williams McCaffrey

Clarion Books
New York

Clarion Books
a Houghton Mifflin Company imprint
215 Park Avenue South, New York, NY 10003

The text was set in 12-point GarthGraphic.

www.houghtonmifflinbooks.com

Printed in U.S.A.

Library of Congress Cataloging-in-Publication Data

McCaffrey, Laura Williams.
Alia waking / by Laura Williams McCaffrey.
p. cm.
Summary: Alia and her best friend Kay long to join the Keentens, a sisterhood of warrior women, but after a punishment caring for captives, Alia begins to question everything that once was certain in her life.
ISBN 0-618-19461-4 (alk. paper)
[1. Sex role—Fiction. 2. Best friends—Fiction.
3. Friendship—Fiction.] I. Title.
PZ7.M122835 Al 2003
[Fic]—dc21

2002008721

QUM 10 9 8 7 6 5 4 3 2 1

For Cerridwyn and Magdalene,
with all my love

And for Colin,
who has taught me so much about
faith and courage

Acknowledgments

Many thanks to my friends and family. Thanks, as well, to the schools and libraries where I've worked over the past five years. A huge thanks to this book's midwives—Susan Bartlett Weber, Mary Gow, Susan Colm, Dale Blackwell Gasque, Deb Abramson, Susan Ritz, Anne Trooper Holbrook, and Robin Sales. Finally, thanks to Jennifer Greene for all her honesty and tact, and for taking a chance.

One

Alia ran swiftly and silently. As she reached a shaggy needle tree, the sound of grunts and cracking twigs came from beyond her. Then, near one of the forest's many thorn bushes, Alia saw a face and a brown tunic. She crouched, hiding herself behind the tree's draping branches.

Alia peered around bunches of long green needles. The face and the tunic were gone. She could see nothing but the silent forest: thick trunks; spindly trunks; dead, hollowed-out trunks. The wind brought her no scent of the other children she knew were close by. Instead, she smelled wood smoke, last night's chill, and something else she had no name for—a spicy scent that the trees seemed to wear when the days grew shorter and colder. But now was no time to close her eyes and smell the fall's breath. No skirmish, not even a mock skirmish such as this, was won by closing one's eyes.

Alia hunkered down on her heels and held herself very steady, waiting. As she listened to the silence, she wondered if a keenten, a warrior woman, might be watching from somewhere among the trees. The warrior women often watched the children's fights and mock battles to see which girls were the strongest, the fastest, the bravest. Then, when these girls reached thirteen springs, the keentens would invite them to join the keenten sisterhood. Unlike boys, who all trained and served for a time as warriors, only girls chosen by the keentens had the honor of learning the war arts and fighting for the village. Alia wanted nothing more than an invitation into the keenten sisterhood, but in the last moons, she had had little time to show the warrior women her worth. Her elder sister had married the past spring, leaving behind all the indoor chores for her. This day was a gift. There wouldn't be many more before the next spring, her thirteenth.

A slight crunching sounded behind her, and she tensed and turned. At the sight of her close friend, Kay, Alia relaxed. She reached out and pulled the tall, leggy girl down beside her.

"It's not good for us," whispered Kay with a grimace. "The Beechians have caught three of our people."

Alia nodded and glanced out into the trees. No real Beechians were hiding out there; this was just how the children named their sides in the mock skirmishes. Alia was a Trantian—one of her own people this time, thankfully. Even if pretending to be a Beechian was simply a game, it still made her feel tarnished.

The Beechians were a foolish, stubborn, savage people. Five falls past, they had driven out almost all their divins—the leaders of their villages—as well as the divins' apprentices. Alia had heard stories of the divins and their families fleeing Beech with little more than packs of hastily grabbed clothes or food. They now lived in exile in Trant or in the mountain province. Even the masters, powerful divins who were selected to advise the Magus, couldn't enter Beech safely. The Beechian masters had to live with the Magus in the capital city.

Since the first autumn of the exile, many men and women from throughout the Magus's provinces, including Alia's two elder brothers, had died while trying to make the Beechians take back their divins and their masters. But the Beechians did not seem to miss their divins' high magic and wisdom, and so the fighting dragged on and on.

Alia shook away thoughts of Beechians and the real war being fought to the north. A keenten must keep her eyes on the battle before her. At least for now, the children's skirmish needed all her attention. "Who's—" Alia stopped, hearing a crackle of branches. She could feel Kay stiffen beside her.

She and Kay looked out into the forest. Not far from their tree walked Alia's two younger brothers. The boys were circling trees and peering into brush piles, as if searching for someone. Alia bit down hard on her lip to keep from cursing. Her brothers hadn't been in the skirmish earlier because Mam had sent them to dig up arrowroots. Before the boys had come to the forest, they might have stopped at the farmhouse. If they had stopped at the farmhouse, they might have seen Mam. And if they had seen Mam, they would have a message for Alia, and Alia already knew what that message would be: Get your backside home.

As the boys walked past the needle tree, Alia held as still as she was able. She was sure they would see her; the stockier, younger one, Temmethy, seemed to look right at her. But as he did, the wiry elder boy, Athon, whispered something in his ear. Temmethy punched Athon's arm, and they started to scuffle. Though the boys' silly arguments usually annoyed Alia, she began to grin. The boys wouldn't look for her again until one of them won the fight. And their fights could last for days.

A cry cut through the forest, and Alia turned

her face toward where she thought she had heard it. She expected to see a waving arm—the sign for the Trantians to attack—but she saw nothing. She waited, then glanced at Kay.

"There," said Kay suddenly, pointing to a different spot, not where Alia had been searching. "Our sign."

Kay sprang up and ran from the tree. As Alia pushed through the needle tree's shaggy branches, she saw that ten or fifteen other children were leaping or dashing or squirming from where they had been hiding. They all ran toward a spot where the ground was level and clear of brush. Alia raced toward the other children, her feet quick and sure.

Ahead of her, Kay stopped as a boy, the Smith's son, blocked her path. The boy had a barrel-sized chest and meaty fists. One moon past, Kay had challenged him to a fight, and though he was no younger than Kay, Kay had knocked him cold. From the hard, determined line of the boy's mouth, Alia expected that he was seeking revenge this day.

Kay struck out at the boy in a series of moves so deft and agile she could have been dancing rather than fighting. Alia watched, respect thrilling through her. Though the girls had been friends their whole lives, Kay's strong, graceful fighting always amazed her.

But not everyone had paused to watch Kay fight. A girl from the Beechian group, Tana, ran forward, grabbed Alia's wrist, and twisted. The pain caused Alia to turn, her arm caught behind her back. Tana pulled up on the wrist, and Alia bent, gritting her teeth.

Tana pulled up harder on Alia's wrist and hissed, "Go down on your knees and yield." Alia bent lower, her head hanging down. She felt ridiculous and stupid. If she had been attentive, Tana would never have been able to touch her. But she swallowed down her embarrassment; it could do her no good now.

Alia bent her knees a bit, as if she were going to kneel and yield. Ever so slightly, Tana's grip loosened. A secret triumph sparked through Alia as she hooked at Tana's legs with one foot.

Tana cried out with surprise and stumbled backward, then sat hard on the ground. Alia straightened and turned in one swift movement, but before she could reach for Tana, something smacked her chest. A thick wetness splattered up onto her face. Laughing and whooping with victory, Tana scrambled up and ran off. Alia looked down and saw the remains of a rotten allam fruit splashed across her woolen dress, chunks tangled in her long black hair. Then another allam soared by her ear. Alia ducked and heard laughter and outraged yells, as well as the thudding of more allams.

Kay rushed over to Alia and grabbed her hand. They started to run.

"No orchards are near this side of the forest. Where could they have found the allams?" Alia asked. As one allam flew by her ear, she saw that it had come from somewhere above, as if thrown from a tree.

Kay said, "One of the Speare boys chose this site for the skirmish. The cheat probably brought the allams before we even began."

Alia and Kay slowed as they left the fight behind them. The Trantians were yelling, the Beechians were laughing; neither group came to look for them. The girls crouched behind some brush. Alia scanned the trees above her.

In a dead tree sat one of Farmer Speare's many sons. The long-limbed boy grabbed several allams from a basket balanced on the two branches beside him. He threw the fruit quick and hard, laughing all the while.

Alia nudged Kay and pointed out the boy. She studied the tree but could see no way to climb it without him spotting her. The basket seemed nearly empty, so she and Kay could wait until the allams were gone before trying to capture the boy, but while they waited, he would keep hitting their companions. Her gaze dropped to the mossy ground beneath the tree. There, by the tree's trunk, she saw another basket piled high with fruit.

Alia pointed to the full basket. "Let's take it," she said to Kay. Kay gave a soft, satisfied laugh.

The girls stepped out from the shelter of the brush. They scooted through an arch made of tangled saplings, then paused and grinned at each other. The boy was too pleased with himself to notice the girls creeping toward him.

They slipped toward the dead tree. Then Kay squeezed Alia's arm as the Speare boy tossed down the empty basket and started to climb down the tree. The girls dashed for the full basket. The Speare boy looked down at them and opened his large mouth.

"No!" he cried and started to slide down the tree, heedless of the branches that cracked and broke in his careless hands.

Kay leapt forward, and Alia was at her heels. Then to Alia's surprise, a small, swift girl, Imorelle, jumped the brush on the tree's other side and sped toward the basket. Alia couldn't remember whether Imorelle was fighting with them or against them. She sprinted as fast as she could, determined not to let either Imorelle or the Speare boy outpace her.

Kay reached the basket first and grabbed one of its handles. Alia arrived just behind her and grabbed the basket's second handle. The boy jumped and landed beside Alia, and Imorelle pulled up hard, almost knocking into him. Both were half a moment too late. Alia and Kay gave victorious throaty yells.

"We've won!" Alia cried out. "We claim your weapons, and the Trantians win."

Imorelle looked as if she'd have liked to yank the basket from Kay and Alia's hands. "If we'd spied out our enemy's plans before attacking, as I suggested, we'd have won sooner." She wrinkled her nose. "And we wouldn't stink of rotten allam."

The Beechians snickered. Alia and the other Trantians glowered at Imorelle. Kay leaned close to her. "Would you really say such things before an enemy?" she whispered in angry exasperation. "You make us all look dull-witted."

"My apologies," muttered Imorelle, sounding mostly, but not thoroughly, repentant. "I was only speaking the truth."

Kay rolled her eyes. Alia shook her head. Every word Imorelle said and every step she took and every fight she fought were for *her* advantage, *her* triumph, *her* glory, even if they might hurt those standing with her. Kay sometimes tried to help Imorelle act with more honor, because she was a great fighter and could be a great keenten. Alia didn't want Kay to fail, but, great fighter or no, Imorelle always rubbed her wrong. But if the keentens chose Alia, and Imorelle, too, she would never disappoint them by showing such feelings.

"Stop whispering, unless you're talking about giving in," said the Speare boy. "Because you didn't win."

The Smith's brawny son hurried over. "We were trouncing you," he said, pointing to Kay. "Before you captured our allams."

"We've taken your weapons," said Kay. She crossed her arms and looked at both boys' dirty faces. "Anyone who wants to challenge me for them can."

Both the Speare boy and the Smith's son glared at her, but despite their hard stares, neither said a word. One corner of Kay's mouth curved upward into a half-smile. Alia's grin stretched from one side of her face to the other.

"We've won!" shouted Kay, and the other Trantians, and even Imorelle, howled their approval.

As the yelling started to dwindle, a voice came from a clump of trees. "I don't know that 'win' is the right word."

The yelling instantly stopped. Alia turned and saw a tall, slender woman step from behind the thick branches. As the keenten walked out of the trees' shadows, she seemed like a warrior woman walking out of the Old Tales—Creanna, or Kris, or Jaline, ancient keentens who had fought heroically side by side with warriors to protect Trantian villages long ago, before the forming of the

Divin Hierarchy and the Magi's rule over all the provinces.

As the keenten, Jen, walked closer, she became more real, but no less glorious. Her face was proud and smooth, and she moved with the lithe grace of a cat. Around her waist was a green sash, symbolizing her oath to marry no man while she ran with the sisterhood. Alia touched the waist of her own wool dress, longing for such a sash.

The keenten stopped in front of Kay. She gestured at the Trantians and said with a sly smile, "I don't think you and your companions won, Kay. Look at them. They're covered in rotten allam."

Alia's cheeks grew hot, and she saw that Kay's cheeks, too, were darkening.

A moment drifted by before Kay spoke. Then the girl held her head high and admitted, "They did surprise us."

The Smith's son and the Speare boy nudged each other and smirked.

"But you did well despite the surprise, Kay," said Jen. Then she inclined her head slightly toward Alia and said, "As did you."

The sound of these words made hope rise in Alia—the wild rushing hope that the keentens would finally want her. Last moon, when the keentens had taken her and Kay and Imorelle and Tana with them to the healers' trade meeting at the Blessed Groves, the same hope had filled her.

But the meeting had gone so strange and then so wrong, turning her expectations painfully sour. Maybe her past disappointments wouldn't matter now. Maybe she had finally, finally proven herself to the keentens.

Alia met the keenten's stare. "Thank you, Jen," she said casually. She didn't want to sound overeager. A warrior woman didn't beg for acceptance.

Jen nodded, her gaze sliding away from Alia's face. "Kay, I'd like to speak with you," she said. She put one hand on Kay's shoulder and led the girl away. The other children began to chatter, but Alia was silent. She watched Jen and Kay, her hope draining away and leaving an ache in her chest.

Jen and Kay walked together, both tall and slender, each dressed in a brown tunic and leggings, each wearing her hair pulled back into a long, thick braid. Jen spoke and Kay nodded; then Kay spoke and Jen laughed long and loud. They looked like two keentens, rather than one warrior woman and an unapprenticed girl. The keentens criticized Kay for picking fights when she didn't have to, but apart from that one small fault, everything she did pleased them. Everything.

"They'll ask her to join them in the spring," Imorelle said to Alia. She, too, stared after Jen and Kay.

"Of course," responded Alia, as if untroubled. She didn't want Imorelle to see her chill fear—fear that the keentens would ask Kay to join them, but not her.

"She won't be the only one," Imorelle said. "Jen talks to me now and again, too." She looked to Alia, expecting, it seemed, Alia's agreement that the keentens favored her as they favored Kay. Whether the keentens favored Alia didn't appear to concern her in the least.

"They'll take whom they take," Alia answered, in no humor to agree with Imorelle about anything. Then she edged away, as if interested in a hole by the root of a tree.

She didn't stop watching Jen and Kay, though. And as she watched them, her hands clenched into fists. She had not been fighting hard enough. She needed to work harder, fight harder, dazzle the keentens. The warrior women had to choose her, as well as Kay. They just had to.

A hand on Alia's elbow interrupted her thoughts. "What?" she snapped. She turned, expecting to see Imorelle, but instead her brother Temmethy stood by her side.

"Mam wants you home," Temmethy said with a big smile. "And she's awful mad."

Two

As they left the forest, Athon said to Alia, "Mam was growling about you running off when we got in from the fields. I bet she makes you scrub the fowl coop."

"That'll take forever," said Temmethy, with a gap-toothed smile. Athon gave a laughing snort.

Alia walked ahead of the boys, her head high. Though she could ignore their stupidity, she couldn't ignore the guilt prickling at the back of her neck. Guilt over Mam. Alia had known Mam wouldn't let her go to the mock skirmish, and so she had asked Papa's permission to join the other children, without speaking with Mam first. But what else was she to do? Kay and Tana and Imorelle were lucky enough to have sisters who helped their mams. All fall and winter, they would be running free in the forests, and the keentens would be watching them—while she was stuck tending her baby sister and scrubbing floors.

Alia dashed through the stalks of newly cut hay, her unhappy thoughts racing faster than her feet. What if the keentens didn't choose her? Except for the Divin's apprentices, all boys learned the war arts and fought the Beechians, no matter if they stayed on their farms or apprenticed with artisans. Only the best boys became spears—men bound to the Warrior House for life—but still, all boys learned and fought for a time. Girls mostly became farmwives, or, perhaps, were apprenticed to artisans or to the healers. Except for the few chosen by the keentens, they never learned the war arts, never fought for peace in the lands. Never. Alia shook her head, tossing back her black hair. She would not let that happen to her.

As Alia neared the hill between her family's farm and Kay's, the sight of someone ahead made her racing thoughts slow. She shaded her eyes against the sun. Standing on the hilltop near the elm tree was a young man. He was skinny and wore a long black robe, which marked him as one of the Divin's apprentices. He raised an arm to catch the children's attention. Alia looked back at her brothers. They both shrugged and began to hurry to catch up. Alia didn't wait for them. She ran toward the apprentice, curiosity speeding her along.

She reached the young man just before her

brothers. He was Bernerd, Farmer Fisker's son—Bernerd Nose-in-the-Air, as her elder sister often called him. "Alia Cateson of the Cateson farm," he said, "the Divin wishes to see you."

Alia's eyebrows raised in surprise. The Divin generally didn't summon her unless some prank she and Kay had played had displeased him, and the girls had played precious few pranks in the last moons: Mam had been keeping Alia too close to home. Alia asked, "Why does he wish to see me?"

"He'll tell you when it's time for you to know," answered Bernerd with impatience. "We should go. I've already spent much of the morn searching for you."

Alia didn't want to follow Bernerd until he stopped looking down at her as if she were a toddling babe. Delaying an apprentice who was on the Divin's errand, however, was not wise. "Tell Mam and Papa I'll be home as soon as I can," she said to Temmethy and Athon.

Athon said, "Don't worry. Mam'll still have a bucketful of things to say when you get there." Alia wrinkled her nose and left him and Temmethy to their laughter.

She went with Bernerd down the hill toward the village. He said nothing to her. As if merely making conversation, she asked, "Did the Divin ask to see anyone else?"

Bernerd wasn't fooled. "He asks to see many people each day," he said, with clear disapproval of the question.

"I suppose he probably wouldn't have told you, anyway. Since you're only an apprentice," Alia remarked. His scowl raised her hopes that she'd knocked his tongue loose, but then he walked ahead of her, refusing to speak again. She let him be, though she thought she might have to drop a fat ten-legged pukeler bug on his neck at the next feast.

Turning her thoughts to the Divin's summoning, Alia trailed Bernerd down into the small cluster of buildings that made up the heart of Loack village. Loack's center was cut in half by the Road, the only well-traveled path leading all the way from the Magus's city in the far east to the Borderlands in the far west. Alia leapt over the Road's ruts and piles of manure. She had to swerve past the Woodworker's frizzy-haired daughter, who was chattering and giggling with the Innkeeper's son.

The Trader's wife was making her way down the Road with her four muddy sons. "Alia Cateson," she called. "How's your dear mam?"

"Just fine," answered Alia without stopping.

Alia and the apprentice hurried over the swaying bridge that spanned the river. On the opposite bank, Alia matched Bernerd's quickening pace and looked toward their destination, the Sacred House. The tall, proud building stood on the hilltop. Its walls were made of thick stone, and though these walls were graced with windows, the sun's light reflected off the glass, so Alia couldn't see into the building. The house, like the apprentice, would tell her nothing of what waited for her inside. She hastened on. It didn't matter. A keenten must be ready for anything.

Bernerd and Alia opened the Sacred House's massive door and strode into the Great Hall, the room where the villagers came to feast or to hold counsel with the Divin. The sun's slanting rays illuminated bright rectangles of stone floor, but most of the high-ceilinged room was dim. Alia blinked, her eyes adjusting to the shadows and candlelight. Standing in the far corner with one of the Divin's other apprentices were the Woodworker, the Rins—the leaders of the warriors—and Farmer Bold, all members of the Village Council. Though they seemed to be talking of something important, she didn't see the Divin with them.

Bernerd led Alia to a low eating table near the hearth and gestured for her to sit. "I'll tell him you're here," he said. Then he left her.

Alia sat cross-legged on the mat and folded her hands, waiting. The moments stretched on, making her more jittery than she wanted to admit. She remembered suddenly that she and Kay had slipped several fowls into the Divin's Tower two moons past, making the Divin's daughters scream to wake the dead. Perhaps the Divin had discovered who had played the prank? Alia tried to suppress a grin. To hear the frantic curses from the Divin's usually perfect daughters had been worth most punishments.

"Alia."

Alia dropped her grin and looked up and up at the tall, broad man before her—Divin Ospar. Everything about him seemed to gleam with the powers that fed his wisdom, the powers of earth and air, water, fire, and stone. His black tunic shimmered with silver embroidery. Down his chest and at his wrists, he wore the Smith's finest silver buttons, their clever pattern making them seem to squirm and writhe. Even the white streaks in his black curling hair glinted when the light touched them.

Hiding her renewed jitters, Alia said, "Bernerd brought me here. He said you wished to see me."

"I do." The Divin sat, all the while staring at Alia with his night-black eyes. Then he said, "I summoned you because I want you to tell me of the healers' trade meeting."

Alia's jitters melted away. He didn't know about the fowls, and she'd done no wrong at the trade meeting. It had been an honor to be asked, along with Kay, Imorelle, and Tana, and she'd tried her best to impress the keentens. Then a strange fire had started in the Blessed Groves, where the meeting was held, and had killed some Beechian healers. The keentens had not even let her close to the fire. After all her hopes for the trip, it had been a cruelly confusing and awful day. She said, "I told you all I knew last moon, when we first returned. Jen had Imorelle, Tana, Kay, and me stay in the clearing. We didn't go near the Blessed Groves. I didn't even see the fire."

Divin Ospar nodded thoughtfully, as if weighing his words. Then he spoke, his tone grave. "When the Magus learned of the tragedy, he sent masters traveling through all his provinces to learn more. And they have learned a great deal, but not enough. As you know, healers' trade is protected by the Sacred Laws; healers from all the provinces may travel and meet to trade in safety, regardless of war. But at this meeting, someone violated the trading truce."

A shiver trickled down Alia's spine. "You mean someone purposely set a fire in the groves?"

The Divin ran one hand across his high forehead, then slowly nodded. "The lawbreakers were all men, and clever men at that. They came to the Blessed Groves dressed as healers from the mountain province—the only place in the lands where men actually choose to be healers. While the other healers were trading with one another in various parts of the Blessed Groves, these men tricked all the Beechian healers into just one grove. They trapped the Beechians with an air spell and called forth fire in the trees. Then the men disappeared before the warrior escorts could reach the burning grove. The spells were strong. No one could save those Beechian healers, or the grove's trees."

The chill went down Alia's back again. A memory took hold of her. While Jen had driven the wagon through a field, away from the failed trade meeting, Alia had watched other warriors and healers loading their carts and leading their nervous mounts away. Her eye had been caught by a Beechian boy and girl standing beside two skittish ponies. The girl had knelt and hugged herself. Then she had tipped back her head and screamed her sorrow at the clouds. Alia heard the girl's anguished scream in her ears again. She felt cold. The healers and grove had not died by accident. Someone had broken the strictest of the Sacred Laws. Someone had used magic to kill.

"Of course, the killers weren't healers, since healers have no stomach for even the most justified of killings, and even the men healers of the mountain people don't have the strength to kill with magic. I fear some of the Borderland Exiles' sorcerers came into the provinces without us realizing it. But we truly don't know." Leaning forward, the Divin said, "I'm speaking to you, and to all from Loack who went to that meeting, for the masters need to know more about the killers. Tell me of every man you saw that day."

"I will," said Alia, her dusky skin rising into gooseflesh. Maybe she had seen the killers that day, passed them on the Road, walked by them in the clearing near the groves. Maybe she had smiled at them or spoken to them, unsuspecting. "As we started out, we saw a group of peddlers," she began.

The Divin swept up one hand. The sound of rushing air filled Alia's ears, and then a slightly transparent vision of the Road as it led east out of Loack hovered above the table. Dawn's earliest rays of light shone on Farmer Kreston's spotted goats, which stood on one side of the Road, and on a cluster of allam trees, which stood on the other. Up ahead was a cart pulled by mules; the man leading it wore a peddler's hat, lumpy and brown like rising bread dough. Alia's hand itched to touch the air-shaped vision. At feasts and festivals, the Divin always showed them the power of air, water, earth, fire, and stone—the roots of all things. But she'd never been so close to such magic before, close enough to lay her hands on it.

"How many peddlers?" asked the Divin.

"Two walked by the cart. One sat inside it." She held her breath as two more peddlers swirled into the vision. "I don't remember how their faces were," she added.

"That's fine. Just tell me all you can," said the Divin.

The vision spun and shifted as Alia described farmers herding their sheep and goats, musicians whistling as they rode on their caravan, children splashing in a pond, delighted with the unusual fall heat—a spell of Fool's Summer. Everything looked so real in the vision, almost as if the journey was happening all over again. The day sped past, then came a brief moment of darkness for the night they had slept in an inn, then morn arrived again. The morn of the meeting. Alia's heart beat faster and her belly clenched as the Road rolled out before her, drawing near to the Blessed Groves.

Alia took particular care describing what she had seen as Jen stopped the wagon at the edge of the forest that surrounded the Blessed Groves. Mountain people's huge saddled birds appeared in the vision, as well as the Beechians' shaggy ponies. The four healers from Loack melted from the vision as they entered the forest, heading into the groves to trade. "Jen led us to a clearing in the forest where the keenten and warrior escorts were waiting for their healers. There were other girls like us there, too, who had come with keentens from other villages." Trantian warriors and keentens accompanied by girls took form, as well as warriors from the mountain province dressed in their long feather-fringed tunics. "There were Beechian keentens and warriors there, but no one talked to them." Short, dark-skinned, pale-haired Beechians appeared, clustered together, apart from the rest.

"Did any of the warriors slip away?" asked Divin Ospar.

Alia thought hard, then shook her head. "No. I didn't see any go. They were all talking and laughing. Then a healer ran into the clearing, shouting of the fire. The keentens and warriors all ran to help, but Jen made me and the other girls swear to stay in the clearing and wait for her. We didn't see anything of the fire." Alia remembered the acrid taste of smoke in her mouth and how she had stepped forward to join the keentens. But she and Kay, like the other unapprenticed girls, had been left behind.

"Are you sure?" the Divin asked. "While you were in the clearing, you saw and heard no one?"

Alia swallowed, her mouth suddenly dry. "No one," she answered, and shame burned through her. She had thought she had heard something, a whispering, like the call of many hushed voices.

Though she had seen nothing that could make such a noise, the quiet chorus had grown louder, filling her head. Then it had ended abruptly, like something silenced against its will. She had gripped the tree beside her so hard its bark had cut her fingers. She'd been certain she had heard strong magic dying—the strong magic of the trees.

But she had been wrong, very wrong. When she had spoken of the sound, Imorelle and Tana had looked at her as if she were an idiot. Then Kay had laughed and told Imorelle and Tana that they didn't know a good jest when they heard one. Shocked, Alia had realized that the whispering had been nothing but her own excitement and fear. Never before had such wild imaginings taken her over. And they never would again. Not if she was to be a keenten.

"Who else did you see as you left the trading meeting?" asked Divin Ospar.

Alia willed her cheeks to cool and rushed on with her story, though there was little left to say. She told of everyone she'd seen as Jen had fetched her and the other girls, and of those they'd passed as they'd started the long, weary trip back to Loack. The day had been old by then, though, and there'd been few travelers besides keentens and warriors rushing their healers home from the trade meeting. Once the day had died away, Jen hadn't stopped at an inn; instead, she'd begged fresh horses from a keenten house and they'd driven on. The dark Road had been empty except for wagons like theirs and cloaked warriors with spears drawn against any lurking danger. Alia would have noticed anyone else. She hadn't slept that night.

After Alia fell silent, Divin Ospar didn't speak at first, only sat staring down at his hands as if they held some answers. Finally, he looked up at her. He said gently, "I'm sorry you were there. The keentens would never have taken you girls to the trade meeting if they had thought someone would break the truce."

Alia didn't like the way the Divin was looking at her, as if she was a small child who needed protection. "Did I give you anything that might help?" she asked.

"I'll have to think on your story again," he said. His face was stern. "We have to find the men who did this horror. But just as important, we must defeat the Beechians swiftly. They refuse to lay down the sword, bringing anguish to all the Magus's provinces, including their own. This is only the latest of many tragedies and deaths—as you know."

"Yes," said Alia curtly. Her elder brothers had been killed in a skirmish in Beech three winters past. Geoffrey Younger and James had taught Alia anything she had wanted to know about fighting and swimming, fishing and hunting, tending crops and setting pranks. Even now, she sometimes forgot that they would never walk through her house's narrow doorway again.

The Divin's voice lowered. "We can't continue to let the Beechians unleash more warfare and fear and pain."

Alia tingled down to her very fingertips. Her brothers, like many others all across the Magus's provinces, had fought to make the Beechians lay down the sword. She would be part of that fight.

Alia left the Sacred House, her feet eager to run down the path into her future, eager for spring and the keenten sisterhood. Her eagerness lasted almost to her house, when the sight of her nearer future made her slow.

Mam was beating out a rug by the laundry line. Each time she struck it, the rug made a loud cracking sound. Thoughts of the Divin and the keentens and the glory of subduing the rebels left Alia. The rhythmic cracking seemed to echo inside her. Usually, beating the rugs was her chore, but she had left her burden of work on Mam's shoulders this morn.

As Alia neared Mam, she took a deep breath, then let it out. "Mam?" she called.

Mam started, then turned with one hand on her chest, as if to still a rapidly beating heart. "No need to come skulking up all silent like that. I'm no Beechian," she said with irritation. She brushed loose strands of silver hair from her forehead, leaving a streak of dirt behind. "So, Alia Cateson, who told you that you could go running this morn?"

"I finished the chores you gave me. So I asked Papa if I could go. He said yes," Alia answered, but as soon as the words left her mouth, she wished she could take them back. What she had said was merely a poor excuse. She had purposely chosen not to go out to the wash bucket to tell Mam that she had finished with the dishes. She had purposely spoken with Papa because he was more likely to let her run. She had purposely left Mam with extra chores on her hands.

Before Mam could speak, Alia said, "It wasn't right. I should have come and asked you what I needed to do first. I won't run off that way again." She met Mam's accusing stare without shrinking.

Mam's mouth twisted as she studied Alia. "Well. The fowl coop does need cleaning, but I don't hear the fowls complaining—yet . . . if you get my meaning. No more running off when there's work to do.

"Now, go get the water from the well. The floors are as dirty as the sheep pen, and you need to tend to them. You'd think those boys could learn to brush themselves down before they walk in the door."

Alia nodded, though the trapped feeling that had surrounded her in the past moons immediately closed in. As she looked out in front of her, she could see the farmhouse, short, squat, and full of chores—floors to scrub, spinning and sewing to finish, clothes and bedding to wash, water to haul, meals to cook, dishes to clean. Each morn brought with its dawning a fresh load of unending work.

Alia turned away abruptly and walked to the shed to fetch buckets. Though she would keep faith with Mam, she would still find a way to catch the warrior women's favor. She simply had to.

Three

Alia grabbed up some snow and let it melt on her tongue as she climbed into the sleigh next to Papa. The winter wind bit her cheeks. Her nose began to run. It was wonderful.

Alia was happier than she had been for the whole of fall. She had worked hard for Mam, helping with the harvest and the trading for winter supplies and the paying of fall tributes to the Divin, as well as with the house chores—but while her hands had been busy, she had thought of the wide azure sky. She had thought of the mock skirmishes Kay told about during visits. She had thought of the keentens watching for new sisters. And she had felt like an animal trapped in a pen.

The worst day had come just before the first snowfall, when Alia was scrubbing winter cloaks and leggings in the huge wash bucket. The water had been warm but was fast cooling in the chill fall air, and her knuckles were cold and rubbed raw. She was trying to squeeze some feeling back into her fingers when Kay came up.

"Alia, come running this morn. You haven't in ages." Kay's black eyes were bright.

Alia wanted to say yes more than anything. She looked sullenly at a sodden cloak hanging over the wash bucket's edge. "I can't."

"Can't you find some way? The keentens are training by the river and Tana, Imorelle, and I have planned a skirmish near there. We challenged some of the older boys, ones who've already started training as warriors. The boys think they'll beat us easily." Kay's mouth twitched at the corners. "They're strutting around and bragging over it.

"Come fight with us. Help us beat them while the keentens watch."

Alia looked at the heap of cloaks and leggings beside her, then over to where Mam was dragging out sleeping pallets and piling up blankets—which would also have to go into the wash bucket. Alia felt like hurling something, something that would shatter. "Kay, look at all this work I have to do. You know I can't leave now."

Kay looked at the wash bucket as if noticing it for the first time. Her bright eyes became grave. "Yestermorn, I heard some keentens praising Tana. And Imorelle makes sure they hear all her triumphs. You have to find some way to run free more often."

"When snow flies," answered Alia. "Mam promised that when snow flies and the harvest is over, I'll have days to run." She picked up a dress and began to scrub it viciously. Who cared if it ripped?

"If only you had a chance now—winter's so far away." Kay kicked the bucket. "Too bad I can't give you one of my sisters."

"Too bad my own sister had to go and marry Eesa Fairson," Alia said as she scrubbed the buttons off the dress. It was a stupid thing to do; she only had to sew them back on later.

After that day, Alia had wanted Kay to tell her what the keentens were saying of Tana and Imorelle, but she also had dreaded what she would hear. Kay and Tana and Imorelle might all win the warrior women's approval while she was stuck at the wash bucket. The thought had made her savage.

Finally, finally, the snow had crept over the land, bringing with it glittering icicles and long, starry nights. Alia had awoken a few morns past, determined to get out soon. She and Mam had agreed on a day, and here it was—Mam was baking bread, but Alia was with Papa in the sleigh, with the horses' noses pointed toward the village. Before she was truly free, she had to run an errand for Mam, which was a bother, but she would finish it quickly. She sat on the edge of the sleigh's seat, willing the horses to move faster.

"Shed roof is leaking again," Papa said.

"Is it?" asked Alia. Her fingers fidgeted with the edge of her cloak.

"Your brothers'll have to fix it again."

"Oh" was Alia's only answer.

Papa didn't say anything more. Alia shifted her feet on the sleigh's pine footboard. Then she shifted them again. Why were the horses so slow?

The horses pulled them through open fields and a small forest. A few scattered farmhouses sat near the sleigh paths, smoke drifting from their chimneys. Alia watched the houses and barns and animals, her fingers tapping the seat. As the sleigh neared Loack's cluster of buildings, she could barely sit still. She leaned forward and scanned the village, hoping to catch sight of Kay or Tana or other children huddled together, planning a skirmish.

Papa interrupted her scheming. "Don't waste all morn with the healers. Bring the potion to me in the Smithy before midday."

"I'll be there as quick as I can," she replied.

Papa leaned toward her so she could see the ice on his mustache and beard. "And see you show those keentens your worth this day."

Alia grinned. "I will."

The horses stopped at the river's bank. Alia

grabbed her pack and snow walkers and jumped to the ground. After waving farewell to Papa, she crossed the bridge, holding tight to its guide ropes and stamping her feet hard to make it buck and sway.

After reaching the opposite bank, she ran up the path. The Herb House stretched on the rise above her, long but not tall and made of rough-hewn wood. To its side was a small run-down building, called the Speaker's Shack, though what that name meant, Alia had never bothered to ask. A great thick oak tree rose on the Herb House's other side, standing by the entrance like a guard. As she neared it, a bundled figure came out of the house and hurried toward her. "Alia," came Tana's voice from the gap between the figure's hood and scarf.

"Greetings, Tana," said Alia, wishing she were free to join the girl right away. Then she noticed Tana was cradling a bottle in her arms. "Are you all right?"

"My sister just has a sour stomach," Tana answered with a laugh. "I'm to be an aunt again."

"Best wishes." Then Alia asked eagerly, "Has anyone started a skirmish this morn?"

"Maybe." Tana shrugged as if she didn't care one way or the other. "I'll be seeing you."

Astonished, Alia couldn't think of what to say. Tana usually talked of nothing but mock skirmishes and how she had fought and whom she had beaten. "Tana," Alia called after her.

The girl raised a hand in farewell but didn't look back. Alia wanted to chase after her but glanced over at the pale yellow sun. She had no time to spare; the morn was flying. Walking backward, she watched Tana but still headed toward the Herb House. As Tana started over the bridge, Alia shook her head, then turned and left Tana behind her.

As she approached the Herb House, the door swung open for her. With a last glance back at the bridge and the now small figure of Tana, she stepped inside the house's warmth. The healer who had opened the door, Mari, said, "Greetings, Alia."

Mari had large dark eyes and curls of hair slipping out the sides of her white veil. She was Alia's distant cousin, and older than Alia by five springs. Alia had never been friends with her. Even when Mari was a child, she had preferred digging in herb gardens to playing with other children. It had been no surprise when she decided to become a healer.

"What brings you here on such a chilly day?" Mari asked.

"Greetings," Alia answered, as light flashing from across the room caught her attention. Two pairs of spectacles glinted on the faces of two gray-haired healers. They stared at her from over their teacups, squinting like flightless mullbirds or some other dull, graceless creature. She looked away from them, wondering why anyone would choose to be a healer.

"My baby sister wails and rubs her ears," she answered. "It's been days since she started, and Mam can't heal her."

"Ears. I see." Beckoning to Alia, Mari started walking. "Ears," she repeated, as if examining the sound of the word.

Mari crossed the room, lost in her own thoughts. Alia trailed behind her, glancing restlessly at the low ceiling, the plain wooden floors, the common blue ivy covering the walls. Why couldn't Mari move quicker and think faster? At this pace, Alia's whole precious day would be wasted.

She followed Mari into the kitchen, where row upon row of shelves covered the walls. Each shelf was filled with ceramic herb pots and corked vials. Drying plants hung from the ceiling beams. Overflowing barrels and bags sat next to the pantry door. A spicy dried-plant smell filled Alia's nose, both tantalizing and irritating her. She was surrounded by things from the outside but still trapped in a small, crowded room.

As Mari pushed aside some dangling motherwort, she said to Alia, "How many is several days? Is it two nights, three nights . . . ?"

"Several days?" asked Alia. "Oh, the baby. This has troubled her for six nights."

Mari stopped. "Six?" she asked. Alia nodded. "And your mam has tried garlic oil and tea of coneflower?"

"Of course. She's had seven live children," Alia said, exasperated. "She knows what to give for ear complaints."

"Does the baby have a burning fever or fluid leaking from her ears?" Mari asked, as if she hadn't noticed Alia's tone.

"No fluid. And she's warm, but not hot."

Mari turned away and murmured to herself, "Definitely yellowroot, velvet leaf, and pokeweed oil. And a strengthening spell woven in as well, I should think." She continued her murmuring as she pushed through the herbrarium door, letting it slam shut behind her, so that it hit the tip of Alia's nose.

Alia glared at the door. Only a healer could forget the person walking behind her because she was so eager to cook up vile-smelling brews—and she was stuck with the healers until Mari finished the syrup. With a vexed sigh, Alia shoved open the door and stepped into the herbarium.

She stopped and stared, her anger lost in amazement.

It was as if she had stepped into midsummer. The herbarium was built all of glass and wood.

Because of this, many villagers complained. Glass was expensive, and tributes paid for the glass's making, as well as its transport from southern Trant. Alia herself had often grumbled with Kay and Papa over the herbarium's high cost. But now she breathed in the smell of moist earth and of flowers' sweetness and thought nothing of tributes.

Alia followed one long shelf, running her hand through mints soft as a baby lamb's ear. She rubbed a leaf between her forefinger and thumb, then raised her fingers to her face and inhaled the scent on her skin. The smell made her hungry. She plucked the leaf and popped it into her mouth. Then she chewed it slowly, like a sweet.

As she continued down the row toward the fire, Alia noticed a small tree that she didn't recognize. It had many branches, all thickly covered with silvery green leaves. The tip of each branch had closed buds that were shaped like morrowsuckle, but larger. She walked closer, studying them.

Then she hesitated. The branches seemed to move, reaching out toward her, their teardrop-shaped leaves trembling. She took a step closer. The buds started to rotate, their tight spirals loosening. Slowly, their petals flared out. Alia's breath stopped. They were as scarlet as the sunset.

In an eye blink, the strangeness ended. The flowers pulled in their petals, as if closing their fingers around something dear. The branches straightened and the buds squeezed tightly shut.

"How did you do that?" Alia asked Mari. She kept looking at the tree, but it sat motionless, as if the blooming had never happened.

"I didn't," Mari answered. "You did."

"Stop teasing. I truly want to know what you did."

Mari shrugged and went back to her herb gathering. "Believe what you want," she said.

There was no understanding healers. Alia walked away from the tree and forced herself to avoid even looking at it, not wanting to become a part of Mari's strange game or jest. She had no time to waste on such nonsense.

At the windows, she wiped water droplets from the glass and peered out. On the river's banks was a flicker of movement. She cupped her eyes with her hands and leaned close to the glass. Training warriors and keentens were walking slowly, almost invisibly, blending with the blowing snow. Mari began to go on about velvet leaf and ears. Alia ignored the healer. She watched the figures by the river. If only she were with them, walking silently in the wind.

"Mari, would you attend the Sick Room?" The unfamiliar voice caught Alia's attention. She looked up and saw one of the healers from the common room, Narisse, standing in the doorway.

"Lily and I are called to a birth," Narisse explained. "The mother lives in the village and is laboring quickly. The married healers are on their farms and won't reach her in time."

Mari answered, "Of course. I can make this syrup in there."

"Illana and our eldress are in Sophia Wood but should return by middle meal," Narisse said. She started to pull on her fingers, as if somehow they had been attached to her hands incorrectly. "That warrior sleeps."

The healer's glance flickered to Alia and then returned to Mari. "I hope you'll have no need to give him another . . . dosing."

"I hope so, too," answered Mari.

Alia looked from the older healer to the younger one. The elder's hands couldn't keep still, and Mari fussed with her veil, trying to push back the unruly curls that had escaped it. Puzzled, Alia waited for one or the other to explain.

But Narisse left without saying anything more, and Mari didn't speak, either. Her curiosity sharpened, Alia followed close on her cousin's heels as she went to collect supplies in the kitchen. Alia studied each herb Mari measured out, but all were familiar—small round chunks of holigold, crumbling dried velvet leaf, chopped coneflower root. Still watchful, Alia trailed close behind Mari as they stepped into the Sick Room.

The smell of illness was not erased by the scent of the lavender growing around the room's edges, but this did not make Mari pause. She walked briskly between the two rows of sleeping pallets, and Alia followed her. A creeping lace vine, which grew in a pot hanging from the ceiling, caught in Alia's black hair. Alia paused to untangle herself and was startled by a hacking cough.

She looked around. The only ailing in the room were two of Farmer Bold's children, old Farmwife Kreston, and a warrior with the close-cropped hair of a newly married man: it was Renald Milter. Renald coughed again, his head lifting from his pillow. Pain contorted his face, but he didn't cry out or complain. Pride surged through Alia and her heart beat fast. One day she would prove herself as strong.

Renald began to hack. The hacking went on and on, filling the room. Alia took a step toward his pallet, then stopped. The coughing paused, but Renald gasped and choked as if coming up from a long spell under water. Though she didn't know what she could do to help, Alia began to walk to him again. Mari passed her and knelt by the warrior's head.

"Are you too frightened to help me prop him up?" Mari asked Alia.

"No, I'm not frightened at all." Alia pulled

Renald up and then supported him as he slumped against her. Her hands felt clumsy and awkward. She hoped she wasn't hurting him.

Renald coughed as if trying to expel something stuck deep in his belly. Mari held a cloth to his mouth so he could spit out what he choked up. From her pocket, she pulled a thin tapered bottle and a small cup. Thinking of the healers' conversation in the herbarium, Alia glanced at the tiny drawings on the bottle's side. The pictured herbs were all ones Mam used when any of the children had a troublesome cough.

Mari poured out a thick brown liquid and fed a cupful to Renald. His shoulders relaxed, and he leaned back onto Alia's arm. His eyes closed.

Alia lowered him. He was gaunt and his forehead was beaded with sweat. But his hands, Alia noticed, were clenched, squeezing the edge of the blankets as if they were the arms of an enemy. A fierce respect filled her. Even in sleep, a warrior fights.

Reluctantly, she stood and left his side. She strode between the rows of sleeping mats and joined Mari by the fire. "Will he die?" Alia asked.

"I don't know. He was wounded badly in the chest, and illness has settled there as well," answered Mari, stirring herbs into a pot hanging over the flames. "He was married just before he went to serve a turn in the Warrior House. He struggles to live, and we do what we can to help him."

Alia studied Mari. "The other healer wanted you to avoid giving him another dosing. Will she be angry that you gave him the liquid?"

"No, that wasn't the thing that worries her," Mari said. From the shelf above the hearth, she took a jar of something slimy, which she began to pour into the pot. "Now I must concentrate and speak the spell just right, or you'll have no syrup for that sister of yours."

Alia wasn't satisfied with Mari's answer. She considered pushing for a clearer explanation—but that might distract her cousin from the syrup. No healer mystery was worth delaying her escape from the Herb House.

She turned away from Mari and watched Renald wheeze and moan in his sleep, as if he was troubled by bad dreams. He rolled so he was facing away from the fire. Kicking at his blankets, he rolled again toward the flames. Then he began to cough.

Each cough tumbled over the next. He woke, but seemed to see nothing before him. He hugged his chest, holding himself together.

Mari rushed to him, and Alia followed her. The coughing subsided and Renald breathed in deeply and desperately several times. Mari held up the cloth to his mouth. He spat into it. Alia reached for his hand but pulled back as she saw the cloth. It was flecked with blood.

Another fit grabbed him, forcing his knees to his chest, squeezing him and robbing him of breath. After it was gone, he panted and shivered, seeming more like a hurt child than a warrior. Alia took his hand. It trembled in hers.

"Hold on to me. You'll be all right," she murmured, as if to a baby. She turned to Mari, about to ask if there was more she could do, but Mari's face stopped her.

Mari looked as if she were halfway in another world, one not near the Sick Room. She put her hand on Renald's forehead, then gently straightened him until he was lying flat on his back. She closed her eyes, her lips moving. Her hands reached out and settled on his chest.

Alia felt something move through Renald. It was strong, like a river fed from the sky's steady rain. And it seethed, as if heated by the earth's fiery belly. It flowed fast, pushing everything from its path. Alia thought she might drown in it.

But then it receded. It pulled away from Alia, away from Renald, leaving behind a lingering warmth.

Renald was still sweating with fever, but his breathing was easier. The look on his face grew peaceful, and then he slept.

Alia continued to hold his hand. It had stopped shaking and gripped hers hard. "What did you do?" she asked Mari, her voice full of awe.

Mari swayed to one side, unable to hold herself steady. She laughed weakly. "Something forbidden," she said.

"But you helped him," Alia said.

As Mari swallowed and nodded, Alia heard the Herb House's door slam. Wooden boot soles clacked angrily against the floor, growing louder and louder. The curtain across the Sick Room entrance swung to one side, and the Divin blew in like a freak thunderstorm, his cape whirling. He came over to Mari. The skin around his eyes and mouth were taut, as if clenched to hold in his fury.

He said, "Healer, I felt that from my tower. You've disobeyed me again."

Four

Mari looked up at Divin Ospar and said in a soft, clear voice, "Yes, I've disobeyed you."

"Come with me," he commanded. One of his hands curled around her upper arm. He led her from the Sick Room, with Alia following several paces behind, walking swiftly to keep up.

The Divin continued across the common room. Mari stumbled behind him, her free hand using anything nearby for support: the wall, a stack of baskets, a shelf. At the common room's low eating table, the Divin loosed her and she sank to her knees. He didn't sit.

Alia stopped to one side of the healer, close enough to hear but not close enough to be taken for a partner to Mari's transgression, whatever it had been. At the sight of Alia, Divin Ospar's glare seemed to sharpen, but he said nothing to her.

"A fire spell," he said to Mari, his words filled with anger. "Mixed with earth and water. But still a fire spell. And one of the Ancients' untried spells, at that."

Alia stared at the Divin, trying to make sense of his words. Healing was more about plants than about magic, and healers had the strength only for smaller spells. But if Mari had discovered a spell in the Ancients' old books that could heal in such a way, why shouldn't she use it if she was able?

"Yes. It was one of the Ancients' spells. And it was a fire spell," Mari answered.

Divin Ospar continued as if she had not spoken. "You know the Magus has forbidden healers to use spells untested by the masters. And fire spells have no place in healers' hands; you don't have the strength for them."

Alia looked to Mari, expecting the healer to explain that Renald had required a potent spell; that the spell had not been beyond her strength; that she thought the Divin wrong. But to Alia's astonishment, Mari said nothing.

"Where's your humility, your respect, your concern?" the Divin asked. A muscle in his jaw began to twitch. "You could have killed that man, burned him from the inside."

Mari just sat and stared, like a lump.

"And her." The Divin pointed to Alia. "She was touching him. She could have been scorched."

Alia stepped forward, unable to hold back her thoughts. "Mari might have done wrong, but she didn't hurt me. And Renald needed—"

"You don't know of what you speak," said the Divin, his voice lashing out like a whip.

Alia closed her mouth and glanced at Mari. Mari wasn't even looking at her. Alia wanted to shake the healer for her spinelessness.

Divin Ospar leaned over Mari. "This is the last time you use forbidden spells. The Eldress may be mistress of the Herb House; but if you break any of the Magus's rules again, it will be me you answer to."

Mari folded her hands in her lap, still silent. Alia crossed her arms and looked away. The Divin was sometimes difficult, but he wasn't unreasonable. He would see the spell's need—if Mari would strengthen her spine and explain herself.

"Where is the Eldress?" the Divin asked.

"In Sophia Wood," answered Mari.

Without a leavetaking, the Divin walked away. As he left, he slammed the door behind him.

Alia turned to Mari in exasperation. "If you think you should be able to use the spell, why didn't you defend yourself?"

Mari put one hand on the table. Her body began to sway with fatigue. "Nothing I say will change his mind. It only angers him further when I speak."

Alia shook her head in disgust. Mari always had been a coward. As a child, she hadn't played fighting games. She had never yelled or argued when other children taunted her. Now she was like all healers, too craven to fight for something in which she believed.

Mari's mouth tightened into a grimace. She leaned against the table and closed her eyes. It was as if she had poured all her strength into helping the warrior. Alia wondered what would have happened to Renald if Mari hadn't been there to tend to him. She hesitated, then asked, gruffly, "The Divin won't banish you from the Herb House, will he?"

Mari's eyes fluttered open and she laughed. "Of course not."

She slowly pushed herself to her feet, still laughing. Alia watched her, her cheeks growing hot. As in the herbarium, she was sure she was the butt of some healer jest that she didn't understand. She stood, stiff and awkward, waiting for an explanation.

Mari offered none. Embarrassment and annoyance swelled in Alia. Why had she felt any sympathy for a healer? Healers were fools. Mari deserved any punishment she received. Blessedly, the syrup was almost finished; Alia only had to wait while Mari bottled it, and then she escaped the Herb House.

Alia walked down the path, away from Mari and healers and forbidden spells. The clouds had disappeared, allowing the sun to grace its realm with some warmth. The wind sang her a greeting from an ice-blue sky. She breathed in the sharp, chill air, and excitement filled her. The rest of the day was hers.

Alia left the syrup with Papa at the Smithy, then ran toward the Inn, where Kay would be waiting. The village was full of bustling apprentices and farm folk and warriors, all wearing their hoods down to bask in the rare winter sunshine. Alia called out a greeting to four Speare boys, who were helping to load a many-toothed plow onto their cart, but her feet kept their fast pace. She felt as if she could soar to the treetops.

"Alia," she heard from behind her.

She slowed and turned, for the voice sounded like Kay's, but it was Imorelle who strode over to her. In the tone of an elder sister checking up on a younger one, Imorelle said, "Where are you headed?"

Imorelle's tone annoyed Alia. "I'm meeting Kay," she responded, half-turning toward the Inn. She raised her hand in farewell.

"Lucky for you," Imorelle said. "One of my

mam's looms needs fixing. You haven't seen the Woodworker, have you? He's not in his house. It's been a wretched waste of a morn."

"I know what you mean," answered Alia. "I really have to go now."

"If a skirmish starts, come find me. I should be somewhere along here," Imorelle said, gesturing to the stretch of artisans' houses.

Alia stared at Imorelle, hardly able to hide her rising temper. Imorelle would never miss part of a skirmish to aid someone else. "Ask the Speare boys—they'll know if anyone's planning a fight this day." Alia nodded toward the boys, who were still heaving at the plow. "I'm late to meet Kay. I'll be seeing you."

"But fight plans change so often. It'll be much easier if you come fetch me after everything's settled," responded Imorelle, as if sure that Alia wouldn't mind missing part of a battle for her sake.

Trying to keep her temper from spilling out, Alia said, "I don't expect I'll have a chance."

"You're not being much of a sister warrior," Imorelle said, frowning.

Alia almost laughed that Imorelle could throw such an accusation. "*You* wouldn't leave a skirmish to fetch *me*," she said.

"I—," Imorelle started. Her frown deepened, but then she looked down at her boots for a long moment. "I might." She looked up again. "I would. If you needed me to, I would."

Alia knew she should be glad that Imorelle would say such a thing. Kay would have been glad. Then Kay would have talked of how strong a fighter Imorelle was, of how she was learning to act with more honor, of how they all, and Tana, too, if she could make herself a bit tougher, would be great keentens together. Alia knew she should be as generous to Imorelle as Kay was; Imorelle was a strong fighter. But Alia didn't trust her.

Still, to refuse to help after Imorelle had spoken those honorable words would be small and mean. Alia stifled an irritated sigh. "If there's a skirmish, I'll find a way to let you know about it."

"My thanks." Imorelle smiled a hungry, hopeful smile. "Maybe I'll grab the keentens' favor today."

Alia understood the hunger and the hope, but Imorelle's selfishness further annoyed her. "Maybe we both will," she said, emphasizing the "we" and the "both." Imorelle nodded, not seeming to notice either Alia's hint or her displeasure. As usual.

They exchanged leavetakings, and Alia left Imorelle. As she ran down the Road, she tried to shrug her ill humor away. This was her day. Her free day. She would not let Imorelle ruin it.

Her spirits rose when she found Kay waiting

on the edge of the Inn's water trough, sharpening her bone-handled dagger with quick, sure strokes. Kay saw her and jumped from the trough. "I discovered something incredible. I can barely believe our luck." She threw the sharpening stone into her pack and hurriedly strapped her dagger around her waist.

"What is it?" Alia asked.

Kay looked over at a man coming down the Inn's stone steps. She leaned closer to Alia and said, "A shelter, within Raven Wood, just south of our keentens' last guard post."

"A shelter?" Alia said. "Whose shelter?"

"I don't know," Kay admitted. "I stumbled on it yestermorn while I was exploring Raven Wood. I saw no one, but it was clean and not overtaken by animals." Her voice grew sly. "But if it's some traveling Trantian's, how come no one in Loack knows of it?"

A shiver of anticipation went through Alia. "Do you think it's a wanderer's shelter?" she asked.

Alia had seen a wanderer only once before. His cloak had been stitched with a star turned down side up, showing him to be a man who didn't believe in the rule of the Magi's One Divinhood. He had had a cut on his cheek given to him by the last villagers who had driven him away. The Divin had let him shelter in the field just beyond Loack, but only after he had promised to leave the following morn. A heady certainty filled Alia. If she and Kay brought news of a wanderer's shelter in Raven Wood, that surely would impress the warrior women.

"It could be a Beechian's shelter," Kay said. She sounded half hopeful, half joking.

"The guards would've let a wanderer come into the wood as long as he said he wouldn't stay. Beechians would never have slipped past them," Alia responded, trying not to sound disappointed.

"True," Kay said, shouldering her pack. She gave Alia a grin. "Still, finding a wanderer's shelter would bring us some honor."

Alia grinned back and began to strap on her snow walkers. Then her grin faded. "I promised Imorelle I'd let her know if there was a skirmish this day. There isn't one, is there?" She didn't want to delay their adventure another moment. Especially not because of Imorelle.

"I don't think so. We could bring her with us," suggested Kay. "I owe her an adventure. She helped me fight off an ambush of Speare boys the other morn."

"We could." Alia hesitated, then spoke bluntly. "I don't want to. We'd have to wait around until she finds the Woodworker for her mam. And besides that, I've already seen enough of her for one day. She was saying things that set my teeth on edge."

Kay laughed. "She's always saying things that set your teeth on edge. She's not so bad, Alia. You just have to tell her when she's being a selfish cobswine and then she stops, most of the time. But—" Kay hesitated and shrugged. "It wouldn't be the same if we had her along. And I don't want to wait for her to chase the Woodworker. Let's invite her to run with us another time."

"As long as I get to call her a selfish cobswine," Alia joked, her happiness restored. Laughing, Kay cuffed her shoulder.

The girls started their trek to Raven Wood, cutting behind the artisans' houses and avoiding most of the villagers. They crossed snow-covered fields that sparkled and gleamed so brightly that Alia had to squint. Her eagerness made her feet light, despite the wood-and-hide snow walkers strapped to her boots and the thick, heavy snow. She and Kay talked a bit but then fell silent, just running.

Soon enough, Raven Wood rose before them, its golden-edged leaves shining in the bright mid-day sunlight. Alia smiled. Woods and groves were special places of power. Within them, divins tried to perform the Ancients' old spells—weather spells, spells to make the harvest flourish in time of drought, spells to turn back flooding rivers.

Healers came to the woods and groves to collect rare herbs. Trees in woods and groves also had their own unpredictable wild magic—magic the divins couldn't understand or change. The grand mams said Raven Wood's magic was mischievous and sometimes hurtful. They told stories of the trees hiding paths so people would get lost, or the branches poking at a person until he had bruises on his shoulders and back. The Divin said these stories were nonsense, but mams still warned their children away from Raven Wood. These warnings, of course, made the wood a treasured spot for children—during the day's light.

Raven Wood was one of Kay and Alia's favorite places to explore. Alia liked how she felt a bit frightened within it, even though the grand mams' stories were probably just tall tales. She tramped faster over the snow, eager to finally reach the wood.

The girls neared the wood's edge, where Alia could see the trees' humped trunks and their knobby roots, shaped like toe-less feet. She looked between the trunks and felt, as she often did, that something was looking back at her. She smiled at the shivery, spooky feeling in her belly, then adjusted the pack on her back and stepped into the wood.

The sun disappeared behind the leaves, and blue shadows embraced the girls. They walked quickly, their snow walkers dragging and shuffling over the thin layer of snow. Before they had gone very far, a rapid thumping made Alia's mouth instantly dry, until she realized it was the beating wings of a startled ridge bird.

"This is no good. If the birds can hear us, anyone near the shelter will, too," muttered Kay.

"The trees are so dense, barely any snow has reached the ground. We don't need the snow walkers," whispered Alia.

The hunched trees peered over Alia's shoulder as she removed her snow walkers and strapped them to her pack. She had to retie the pack's ropes twice because her fingers twitched and jumped.

When they had finished, the girls ran quietly past trees twisted like an old woman's hands. Soon, Kay whispered that they were near the shelter. Alia slowed, her body tense and alert.

"There it is," whispered Kay, pointing.

Alia could see the shelter clearly. Rocks encircled a fire pit. Woven branches were pulled over the roots of an upended tree, forming a small cave.

And a tattered cloak hung from a sapling.

Alia exhaled slowly until all the breath left her. The cloak was green, and white fur dragged from the hem's torn lining. No one in Loack, nor any travelers through the village, wore the white fur of the northern animals. She was here, in Raven Wood, with the enemy.

The sound of rushing blood filled her ears. She had found what she had hoped for and sought these long moons. Something for which the keentens would give her high praise. Something to convince them to choose her.

"A Beechian," said Kay softly.

"Do you think he's inside?" Alia whispered. The wind caught the cloak and shook it. Alia listened for something other than the thwack of the cloak's rhythmic flapping. She heard nothing. Now they should go find a keenten or a warrior. They should—but Alia didn't move.

"We should see if we can glimpse him," said Kay. She wore the mischievous smile she always wore when she proposed something a little dangerous.

"But we can't let him find us," said Alia, glad that Kay felt as she did. They would stay until they made sure the enemy hadn't abandoned the shelter and the cloak. Then they would fetch the keentens and share in the glory of the warrior women's respect. "Let's hide in the trees."

They climbed onto the lowest of a tree's upper limbs, then sat so they could see the shelter clearly. Alia strained to hear oncoming footsteps and tried to think of a plan. In all the Old Tales, great warriors and keentens always had plans.

"We should think of what to do when we see them," Alia said.

Kay answered, "From this distance they won't notice us. It'll be like spying on the Village Council meetings from the Sacred House windows. When we've seen enough, we'll slip away, just like when we slip over the Sacred House's garden wall."

Kay seized Alia's hand, and her next words came out in a rush. "But I wish we were already initiated. Then we could capture him ourselves."

Alia thought of what it would be like, coming into the village with a prisoner tied behind her. Imorelle, Tana, the Speare boys, and all the artisans' children would line the Road to watch. The Innkeeper and the Trader's wife would gossip of her bravery. The keentens would speak to her in a new way, the way they spoke to Kay, the way they spoke to a sister.

"Next winter we'll take part in attacks," Kay promised.

"I hope to," said Alia. Once she said it, she wished she hadn't. She hoped Kay didn't think her too desperate for the keentens' favor, like an annoying, overeager puppy.

"You shouldn't worry," Kay said, squeezing Alia's hand. "They'll be sure to take you."

Alia squeezed Kay's hand in return, a fierce

resolve surging through her. They would never be separated. The keentens would take her. As sisters, they would fight side by side for justice and glory.

The friends watched the shelter as they nibbled a meal of bread and cheese. They saw and heard no one, though, other than the occasional tree mouse or trengdeer or bird. The waiting dragged on. Stiffness claimed them, and their hands grew painfully cold in their mittens. The shelter looked deserted, and the shadows were growing long.

"Let's just peek inside and then go tell the keentens what we've found," suggested Alia.

Kay nodded, and Alia started to shinny down the tree. Then she halted: a strange birdcall flew through the forest. An answering call came from within the shelter's woven branches.

Within the shelter. Someone had been inside it all this time.

Kay helped Alia ease back onto the tree branch. The two girls looked at each other, then stared down at the shelter, waiting for warriors to appear. Alia feared the sound of her shaking breaths would betray them.

A girl who looked about Alia and Kay's age stepped out of the shelter. Her light hair and dark skin marked her immediately as a Beechian.

A boy of about the same age emerged from

behind a tree. He was thin and gangly, with brown hair tied back from his dark-skinned face. He held a dead fowl and a loaf of bread in his hands.

"Children?" Kay whispered. "They may be apprenticed, but they can't be old enough to be fully initiated into keenten and warrior houses. Do you suppose the Beechians are so desperate, they use children as spies?"

"Where are their weapons?" asked Alia. She watched the Beechians closely. She saw no spears or bows. The boy and girl didn't even have daggers around their waists. They could be wearing them elsewhere, perhaps in their knee-high laced boots.

"I don't see any from here," answered Kay. She leaned as far as she dared from the tree to look.

Alia knew what Kay was thinking. She wanted to say it first. When Kay righted herself, Alia whispered in her ear, "Let's steal a closer look."

Alia and Kay slipped down to the ground and crept toward the shelter. They circled behind the fallen tree, then crouched behind the wall of earth and roots that formed the back half of the shelter. They peeked through gaps in the crumbling dirt. The spies were standing by their fire pit, speaking in their strange whistling language. Alia studied them, her heartbeat again thundering in her ears.

"I see their bows by that tree," Kay murmured.

"And a knife is on the ground by the fire pit," Alia answered. Two bows and a knife, hardly any protection at all, especially since she and Kay had the advantage of surprise. She thought of the way the keentens would look at her as she presented the prisoners.

Kay seemed to know her thoughts, even though she hadn't spoken them aloud. "If we block their path to the bows, we can take them easily," said Kay. Alia could see the battle glow rise to Kay's thin face. Her own blood was rushing to her cheeks and neck, warming them. "Take my dagger and grab the girl," Kay continued. "I'll fight the boy."

Alia took the dagger, for now was no time for foolish pride. She was quick, but not always strong enough to overpower an accomplished challenger. Kay had less need for a dagger; her body was her best weapon. Alia gripped the dagger's bone handle firmly, heat and cold flooding through her, each chasing the other.

When the Beechian girl walked over to the shelter's entrance, Alia and Kay burst into the little clearing. Alia grabbed the girl's hair and pulled. The girl yelled, and her hand lashed out, almost hitting Alia in the neck. Alia tripped and fell against the shelter. The Beechian clawed at

Alia's hand. Alia yanked the hair harder. The girl bent backward like a bow.

Alia pulled her enemy close, touching the dagger to the girl's throat. The blade gleamed like a savage tooth near the girl's fluttering pulse. Alia had helped kill animals before—fowls, felar cats, trengdeer. But this pulse was different, too like the pulse of her sisters, of her brothers, of Kay. Alia's hand shook. She thought of Mam and Papa, her married sister, her brothers, her baby sister—all unaware that Beechians were sneaking near them. All in danger because of this girl. The shaking left her and she held the knife steady against the girl's smooth neck.

Alia looked toward Kay and the other Beechian. "Boy. I've got your girl," she called out, though she realized after she said it that he might not understand.

The boy turned his head, though, and when he saw the girl, he immediately stopped fighting. Kay had not expected him to give in so easily. She had already started a kick that hit his face while his hands—one of them holding a knife—dangled at his sides. He fell to the ground, the thin layer of snow splashing over him.

Kay took his knife and jerked him up. She unlashed her snow walkers from her pack and used the twine to bind his hands. Alia pushed the girl toward Kay. Then she took a good look at her enemy.

The girl's hair was shaggy. She wore a leather pouch around her neck, as all Beechians did. It was the only thing she wore that looked well tended.

Though the boy's hair was brown, his eyes were yellow, marking him a Beechian as well. From the trees he had looked tall, but he wasn't. He was lanky like a big man, with long arms and big hands, but he was shorter than Kay. Strapped around his waist was a slender flute, an odd thing for a spy to wear. A bruise was growing around his eye. Part of his cheek and upper lip looked puffy.

A jolt went through Alia. She and Kay had captured Beechians. She wanted to scream her triumph to the edges of the land, but didn't. She held the scream in, not making the mistake of letting down her guard in front of the prisoners. Still, triumph burned inside her like a raging bonfire.

Kay finished tying the boy and girl, then asked, "Do you speak the provinces' Common Speech or only your Beechian pig language?"

The boy pulled back his head as if Kay had kicked him again. The girl didn't even blink her pale green eyes.

"We speak both Leaf and Common Speech," the girl answered.

"Leaf Speech, is that what you call it? As bad

as healers," Kay said. "It's a wonder you have any warriors."

Alia laughed and walked forward, preparing to start the journey home. But to Alia's surprise, Kay put a hand on her arm, stopping her.

Kay strode to the prisoners. She put her face close to the girl's. "So what are you doing here?"

"Collecting herbs," answered the girl.

Kay laughed harshly. "How stupid do you think we are? Collecting herbs? In winter? In our lands?"

The girl didn't say anything. She studied Kay as if no question had been spoken.

"Shall I describe what we do with spies?" asked Kay.

Alia stared at Kay with growing apprehension. She had seen Kay provoke fights before; Kay would strike with her words, trying to get someone to hit her first. The prisoners' hands were already tied, though.

"And what a beautiful meal you have here. One thing this war has proven—Beechians are terrible thieves," Kay taunted.

"Take it." The boy's tone was accusing. "Do what Trantians do best—take from those less able to fight back."

Kay's knees bent, bringing her weight low. "It's easy for you to insult my people with your hands bound, boy. You know I'd shame myself to strike you now. But what if I cut you free?" Her voice dropped, but each word was clear. "Would you be so eager to speak then?"

Alia bit down on words she wished she could snap at Kay. Kay *had* to provoke the Beechians, *had* to have one more chance to put a bruise on the boy's face. Night was coming, the boy was no true threat, and they were going back to receive the warrior women's praise; but Kay was too caught in the glory of giving another kick to an enemy to see clearly. Alia willed Kay to open her eyes and see her foolishness, so they could get back to the Keenten House.

Kay waited, half-smiling, for the Beechian's answer. Alia's whole body tensed as she watched the boy look sideways at the girl. The girl shook her head slightly—no. Alia exhaled through still-clenched teeth.

But the boy's face was full of defiance as he looked back to Kay. His chin tilted up. "Cut me free."

Kay grinned and reached out so Alia could hand her the dagger.

Five

Alia held the dagger close so Kay would have to come forward to take it. "You don't need to fight that boy. He's no threat to either of us," Alia said urgently, keeping her voice low. "And dusk is coming. We've no time for this."

"We have time enough," Kay said, taking the dagger from Alia's hand. Her expression hardened. "That boy needs to learn some respect."

Kay turned away, and the battle glow returned to her face as she approached the boy. He stood very still, his bound hands offered to her.

Alia's thoughts raced. She had to find a way to stop Kay without making them both look like fools. As Kay reached the boy, Alia started forward, though she still had no idea of what to say or do. Then she halted in mid-stride. Unearthly screeches seemed to come from all around her. They swirled, rising and falling, then rising again. Their shrillness pierced her, shaking her bones. She looked wildly about for whatever creature could possibly be making that noise.

Then she noticed the others and she gaped. Kay's head was tilted, as if she were trying to hear words spoken from a long way off. The Beechian girl glanced up and around, then looked back to the boy and Kay, her hands rising to hold the pouch around her neck. The boy stood unmoving, his bound wrists still outstretched toward Kay. They all heard something, but only Alia seemed to hear the bone-shaking screams.

She tore her gaze from the others and looked to the wood. She saw nothing but humped, twisted trunks. Fighting the urge to cover her ears, she asked Kay, "Do you hear that?"

She could just make out Kay's answer through the shrieks. "A strange bird," Kay said.

Alia stared at her friend in disbelief, but Kay was not jesting. Alia searched the thick fingerlike branches above her. "It doesn't sound like a bird to me," she said sharply.

Kay shrugged, but she, too, looked out into the looming trees and the shadows. "An animal, then." She was silent a moment, squinting into the wood. Then she tossed back her braid and pointed her dagger at the boy. "The day is further along than I'd thought, boy. We need to get you back to the village. But don't worry, your honor will be tested often enough once we get there."

To Alia's amazement, the shrieking broke off. No one seemed to notice its absence but her. Kay gathered up the prisoners' weapons. The boy pulled back his hands with a scowl. The girl watched them all, her feelings hidden away. Alia breathed deeply, expanding muscles that had been pinched by the shrillness. She took a step toward the clearing's edge, searching the trees once more.

She saw nothing, not even a bird or tree mouse. A shiver rippled down her spine. Perhaps the grand mams were not so wrong about the strangeness in the wood. But why had she heard the screaming clearly, while the others hadn't?

Then Alia caught sight of the boy staring sullenly at her. To speak her questions before the prisoners would not be wise. They might think her weak or distracted or an easy dupe. She made her face blank and smooth, as if the screaming had never happened.

She walked over to help Kay, who was tying a Beechian bow to her pack. As Alia knelt, Kay whispered, "You were right about the dusk, but I wish I hadn't noticed." Kay yanked hard on the twine. "That Beechian deserves another thrashing."

"What would the keentens say if you thrashed him?" Alia whispered back, her irritation interwoven with disquiet. Kay's words made it seem as if no sound had caused her to stop and notice the dusk, as if no sound troubled her as it troubled Alia.

Kay's cheeks went red. "He wanted to fight," she said, her voice low but angry.

Alia bit back a retort, knowing she shouldn't argue in front of the prisoners. The silence was retort enough. Kay's face flushed deeper, as if she realized her excuse wasn't one the warrior women would have accepted. She nodded, a jerk of the head. "You're right. I acted with less honor than I should have."

Alia shrugged, gratified. Then she rose, wanting to hasten away from the wood and toward the keentens. "Let's get to the Keenten House."

While Kay tied on the Beechian girl's cloak, Alia searched for their snow walkers but found none. She strapped on her own and readjusted her mittens and cloak against the cold. A wind blew through the wood. Crooked branches creaked and swayed. Alia watched them from the corner of her eye. She wished that she had the power, lost since the time of the Ancients, to make the air carry her and those with her, so they needn't walk back among the twisted trunks.

They left the little clearing and followed a weaving path. The boy kept their pace slow—purposely, Alia thought. He walked with an odd shuffle, as if he wanted to snag his boots on every fallen branch and dead log. Indigo shadows settled around them, making the trees' trunks seem more gnarled and ugly. Alia didn't like the way they looked at her. She took the boy's arm and forced him to walk faster. "Come on, clumsy," she said. He scowled at her, but she pretended not to notice.

After tramping on a ways, they finally stepped out of the last tier of trees into early eve's welcome light. As Kay walked on, Alia couldn't help but cast a last quick look at Raven Wood. It stood tall and silent, its leaves glowing golden against the deep blue sky. A memory that had bearing on its strangeness tugged at Alia—a bit of gossip? A story? She couldn't catch the thought. She turned her back on the wood and started toward the village.

They pushed through the snowy fields, and soon Alia could see the peaks of the village's roofs ahead of her. Raven Wood's strangeness dwindled in importance; ahead of her was glory. If she and Kay beat the darkness, they could take the prisoners the long way to the Keenten House, through the village center. Everyone would stop and stare. The Divin's lessons to his apprentices would end. The Potter would neglect her clay and wheel. The Smith would leave his fires to stand in his doorway. All would cheer as she and Kay led the Beechian captives. If they hurried.

Kay must have been thinking the same thing,

because she began to prod the prisoners forward. The snow was deep outside the wood's shelter, though, and the Beechians seemed to be tiring. Alia and Kay began to pull them along, hauling them up when they slipped or sank to their knees.

Alia spied Farmer Rilterson's stone wall not far from them. "Over to the wall," she said. "The snow has blown off the stones. We can walk easier there."

At the wall, Kay bent to remove her snow walkers, while Alia guarded the Beechians. Alia glanced at the violet sky and tapped her toes inside her boots, silently urging Kay to hurry.

Suddenly, something wet and cold blinded her. *Snow*, she thought, uncomprehending. She raised her mittens to her face. *Someone has thrown snow at me.*

Two large, strong hands grabbed her wrists. Alia blinked her watering eyes and shook her head, while the boy shouted something in his own language. Then he said to her, "I'm not always clumsy, you little tyrant."

A hot rage burned through Alia. Tyrant? He was a ragged, thieving, traitorous spy. What did he expect? That she would welcome him here? Show him her home? Watch him destroy the rest of her family? She would never let that happen. But none of her thoughts reached her mouth. All she said was "Let me go."

The boy only held Alia tighter with his still bound hands. She pushed at him to upset his balance. He didn't move. Alia's feet were trapped in the unwieldy snow walkers, rooted to the ground. She bent, trying to clamp her teeth on the skin peeking out from the boy's unraveling sleeve cuffs. He yanked her arms over her head. She had to stand there, furious, with her arms stretched to the sky.

She met his gaze squarely, ready to let all her thoughts tumble out and smack him on his already bruised face. But the words shriveled in her mouth. No one had ever looked at her that way before. His expression paralyzed her, etching itself into her memory. Anger. Hatred. Disgust. The Beechian boy didn't think himself evil or wrong; he thought she was.

The sounds of fighting broke through the boy's and Alia's locked stares. The boy looked away, to the girl and Kay. Alia's rage surged back. She spat, aiming for the smooth skin of his golden-brown cheek.

The boy swerved and Alia's spittle missed him. His angry look turned back to her. She tilted her chin up proudly.

A triumphant yell startled them both. Alia turned her head and saw Kay pulling the girl toward the wall. Snow clung to their clothes and hair. The girl's face looked as if it had been chiseled from stone. She stared straight ahead.

"Let go of my friend, or I'll stab your girl," said Kay. She grinned. "You know I would if I had to."

The girl's expression didn't waver. The boy squeezed Alia's wrists until all her fingers tingled. Then he let go.

Wordlessly, his face closed up like a shuttered window, the boy held out his tied wrists to Alia. She pushed him toward the wall, touching him as little as possible. With dusk falling so fast, they now would have no chance to parade through the village, but Alia didn't care. The sooner the wretched boy was off her hands, the better.

Alia removed her snow walkers as Kay, with dagger drawn, watched the prisoners. When Alia was done, Kay dragged the girl behind her, walking on the wall's icy stones with feline grace. Alia clambered onto the wall after the boy. She fixed her glare on his cracked boot soles. The boy pretended to stumble and slip often, trying to provoke her into some stupidity, some misstep that would give him a chance to escape. Alia hid her annoyance and did nothing. He wouldn't dupe her again.

The group hurried while the sun sank fast behind the mountains. When they reached the curving section of the wall, they all hopped into the snowdrifts, then waded over to the path that ran between the Keenten and Warrior Houses. Alia could see the Keenten House ahead; a long low-roofed building. Excitement prickled the hair on the back of her neck.

Kay and Alia made the prisoners stand side by side in front of the Keenten House's door. Kay raised her hand and rapped hard against a majestic carving of a sword. Though eagerness jittered through her, Alia tried to hold herself still and dignified. She straightened her cloak and stared at the door carvings: intricate ivy patterns sprouting not leaves but swords, spears, and daggers.

The door swung open, and Jen, the keenten who had brought the girls to the healers' trade meeting, stood in the doorway. Surprise arched her eyebrows and pulled open her mouth.

"Where did you find those?" she asked.

"In Raven Wood," answered Kay. "Alia and I found a shelter and when we saw these two, we captured them and brought them here."

The keenten's eyes narrowed. She studied them all without speaking. Alia's anticipation faltered. This was not the greeting she had expected.

Jen said, "Wait here a moment. I'll help you lock them up." Then she disappeared inside, shutting the door behind her.

Jen didn't return quickly. As the moments dragged on, Alia's stomach twinged with unease.

Why were she and Kay not receiving a glorious welcome?

When Jen finally joined them, any surprise she still felt was hidden. Holding a lit torch before her, she led them past the Warrior House to the Prisoner House. Alia watched Jen's braid as if some clue to the warrior woman's thoughts could be found there. The thick braid swung back and forth at Jen's waist, confessing no secrets.

When they reached the stone prison, Jen pulled open the door. They walked into the windowless darkness. With her torch, the keenten lit two candles on the wall by a fireplace. Then she led the way down the narrow, drafty hall, lighting lanterns as she went. She pulled open the door of the last cell, revealing a stone room with close walls and a low ceiling. It smelled dank, like stagnant water. She nudged the Beechians into the cell. The boy stumbled and grabbed the barred door, as if to keep himself from falling.

Kay laughed, the sound echoing through the Prisoner House. Alia let out a loud "Ha," amazed that the boy would still try to hinder them. The keenten looked sharply at the girls, her expression disapproving. Kay's laughter stopped short. The unease in Alia's belly congealed into a frosty lump.

Jen slammed and locked the door. "You both follow me. Your parents have been sent for."

Alia and Kay trailed the keenten back to the Keenten House. Alia tried to catch Kay's attention, but Kay walked on, unnoticing and seemingly unconcerned. Alia couldn't push her worry away. It clung to her with tenacious, unpleasant fingers. She drew her spine straight and strode on, trying to ignore its grip.

Jen took them to the common room. Alia had long wished to be invited into the house's common room, but what she saw didn't cheer her. The simple room was empty—no welcome party sat there. And Jen left them without so much as a smile or an invitation to warm themselves by the fire. Alia sat on the woven rug. Kay stood before one of the walls, studying the hides with odd lines drawn on them that hung there.

"I think we've displeased her," Alia remarked.

"Maybe," said Kay without turning around. "But how can she really be angry when we've brought the house two prisoners?"

Alia had no answer. She looked out the one small window, and in the last remnants of the sun's light, saw twelve keentens coming toward the Keenten House. A tall, willowy woman strode before all the others. She wore the blue head scarf that marked her as a Rina, a keenten leader. Behind the keentens were Kay's parents and Mam and Papa. Not one of the group was smiling.

The keentens entered the room without making a sound. Behind them came the girls' parents. Papa and Mam stared gravely at Alia, but the keentens worried her more. All of them wore their mouths in hard, straight lines. She saw no hint of praise in their faces.

The Rina, named Eleri, stood in front of the girls with her legs apart and her arms folded across her chest. Everyone else sat straight-backed and cross-legged around her. She spoke in a soft, clear voice. "Your parents were worrying over you. They came to the village for news of you. Then you appear here with two Beechian children. We'd like to know what happened."

Kay started the story as if she were already a warrior woman and had come in to report a successful attack. The Rina interrupted her.

"So you found the shelter yestermorn, not this day. And you told no one?" the keenten leader asked, her words clipped short.

After a brief hesitation, Kay answered, "Yes, but I didn't know anyone was at the shelter." She glanced over at Alia; for the first time, Alia saw doubt flicker across her friend's face. Alia's throat grew tight.

Kay continued as if the Rina had not interrupted her. When she described the girls' arrival at the shelter and the Beechian cloak, Rina Eleri stopped her again: "You knew an enemy was near the shelter, maybe even in it. Once you knew this, you could have fetched a trained warrior. But you chose not to?"

"Yes," answered Kay, wearing the impassive expression she used when she wanted no one to know she was upset.

The tightness in Alia's throat began to ache. She suddenly felt enormously stupid. Keentens or warriors would not have had to struggle to capture the Beechians. They never would have given the boy and girl any chance to escape. In not fetching the trained warriors, she and Kay had been foolish, glory-blind idiots.

After Kay finished her story, the Rina raised one hand, and the keentens stood. "I've heard enough for now. Wait here," the Rina said to the girls and their parents. Not one of the warrior women looked back as they filed from the room.

When they had gone, Mam fumed, "Of all the ox-headed, fowl-witted daughters . . . "

"Reckless," Papa added with disapproval.

"Kay, you're forbidden to range on your own," said Kay's mam. Kay's expression didn't change, though Alia could see her lower lip quiver slightly. "Don't depend on being able to again before spring."

"No more roaming for you, either," Mam said to Alia. Alia sat very still. The winter stretched before her like a wasteland. "I can't imagine what you were thinking. A ridge bird would've had more sense."

"You'll be shoveling slop from the barn through the spring thaw," promised Papa. Alia nodded. At least she would be in the shed with the animals.

"And," Mam said, as she folded her chapped hands in her lap, "every moment you're not in the barn, you'll be sitting inside, beside me, mending anything with the smallest rip, until planting time."

Alia's eyes stung. "I understand," she said, proud that her voice didn't waver.

Then the door creaked open. Alia turned her head to watch the keentens enter. As she saw the line of erect warrior women, a stark thought hit her, making any other punishment seem insignificant. Maybe the keentens would shun her and Kay, ending all possibility of the girls' joining the sisterhood. They had done it to other girls. Alia stared at the keentens without blinking. They couldn't. They just couldn't.

The warrior women seated themselves in one fluid movement, as if they were all a part of the same body. Rina Eleri remained standing and gestured for Alia and Kay to rise.

"Sometimes the measure of a good warrior is that she knows when to turn back. You have both shown yourselves lacking," said the Rina.

Fear made Alia's heart pound. Her palms

were clammy. She couldn't look away from the Rina's beautiful, fierce face.

"Your parents will discipline you in any way they see fit, but we will also require two things of you. You will clean out the stalls of the warriors' horses and the Divin's family's horses, as well as any horses kept by the Divin's apprentices," said the Rina.

Alia nodded, barely hearing. This was obviously the easier of the two requirements.

Rina Eleri continued, "You will do this all winter and through the spring thaw. The stench on your boots—"

"And leggings," offered Jen with a feral smile. "And cloaks."

The Rina raised one eyebrow, and the smiles that had crept over a few of the keentens' faces disappeared. Then she said, "The stench will follow you after you've left the Stables. I hope it will remind you to think."

Alia and Kay waited. The mirth had whisked from the room, leaving a chill behind it.

The Rina stood taller, her expression unreadable. She said, "However, we're impressed with your daring."

Both Alia and Kay straightened, like trengdeer startled in a field. It took a few moments for the words to sink through Alia's skin. When they did, she had trouble catching her breath.

"A daring fighter needs to learn responsibility to become a superior warrior," said the Rina. "Our second requirement involves the prisoners. Until their fate is decided, you're responsible for feeding them, changing their bedding, and cleaning their slop bucket."

The woman looked at them speculatively. "Don't disappoint us again."

Kay looked to Alia, her face full of delight and triumph. Alia smiled back, wanting to laugh and cry and shout all at the same time. They would face this test together. And together they would pass it.

Six

The next morn, the Divin called a Village Council meeting so his councilors could advise him on the matter of the prisoners. Alia wanted to go and watch, but Mam ordered her to stay home and keep the baby and the boys out of trouble. The stern expression on Mam's face called forth the memory of yestereve's scoldings, and Alia didn't argue.

All the morn, Alia tried to imagine what was happening at the meeting. The councilors would sit by the Divin; the Rinas and the healers' Eldress on his right, and on his left, the warriors' leaders, the Rins, as well as the spears—the best warriors, who were chosen to serve all their lives rather than only every third cycle of seasons. The artisans and the heads of the largest farm families would sit facing the Divin. The rest of the Sacred House's Great Hall would be filled with villagers. Maybe even some who lived on the outlying farms, like her sister, Sarian, would be there. What were they all saying? What would the Divin decide to do with the prisoners? These questions buzzed in Alia's head so she could barely keep her attention on the wandering baby, who had the bad habit of squirming out of her leggings and soiled wrappings. Alia had a great many messes to clean. Athon and Temmethy avoided the house.

Finally, after midday, Alia heard a horse whinnying on the path. She scooped up the baby and went to meet Mam and Papa at the door.

"You'll be wanting to know what happened," Papa said to Alia as he took off his cloak.

"What did they decide?" asked Alia.

"Not much, for all the talk, talk, talk," said Mam, reaching for the baby. "Some want the prisoners executed—like any other spies. Some want them questioned by the keentens. Some want them sent to the Magus's city, to drudge in homes or workhouses or mines. You should have seen the fight between the Innkeeper and her husband over it. I thought she was going to smack him, until the Divin told them both to hush.

"The Divin finally decided to send a message to the masters asking for their guidance. He won't do anything until he hears a reply." Mam shook her head. "It's a sorry situation. I can't imagine what kind of people would send unapprenticed children out as spies. Even those who're trained and know the war arts aren't sure to be safe."

Mam's face was suddenly pinched and unhappy, and Alia knew that she was thinking of James and Geoffrey Younger's deaths. Alia shifted uncomfortably. She didn't like it when Mam's grief came all of a sudden, sometimes with tears that no one could stop, and she didn't like it when Mam talked of nothing but the loss in war, as if there were no gain.

Papa reached over and squeezed Mam's hand. "None of us will be safe until we defeat the Beechians. Which we will." Mam made the effort to smile, and Papa smiled back. "And," he added, "our girl will help. The Divin wants to see you this eve, Alia—you and the keentens. He has something he wants you to do for him."

"Does he?" Alia asked, eagerness overrunning her worries about Mam. "What is it?"

"He didn't tell us, though he was quite impressed with your bravery," Mam said, her pinched look easing. Alia grinned. "You'd better not let praise start swelling your head, though, or you'll have me to answer to, bravery or no bravery," Mam warned.

Alia's grin broadened. "I won't."

The day couldn't go by fast enough for Alia. She worked and paced and paced and worked until, at long last, the sun hung low over the mountains. Then she met Kay, and they rushed to the prison with food for the captives, eager to be done with their chore quickly and on their way to answer the Divin's summoning. The Beechians ate their stew and bread, sitting sullen-faced and silent the whole time. The cell was dim and cold and stank, even after Kay emptied the slop bucket. Alia was so impatient to leave, she could barely stand still. Once they were finally outside again and racing down the path, everything suddenly seemed beautiful to Alia: the clouds rippling over the sky, the feel of her legs taking her forward, the taste of the air.

As she and Kay came around the Loom House to the Road, they saw Imorelle sitting on the house's steps, watching the path as if she'd been waiting for them to come by. She hailed them, her expression brooding and dour. Alia stiffened. Imorelle probably thought that Alia'd wronged her by not inviting her on the adventure to Raven Wood. As if she had to be invited to everything, as if no one should do anything but help *her* win glory. Alia went forward, readying herself to trade hard words.

Imorelle put on a smile that made her look no happier and said in a flat voice, "So, you've won your invitations, for certain."

Kay nodded. Alia answered, "Probably. We

have to tend to the captives as a final test." Then she waited for Imorelle to say what she really wanted to say.

To Alia's shock, several tears spilled down Imorelle's cheeks. Imorelle wiped at them, obviously frustrated that she hadn't been able to keep them from falling. "Good luck to you both," she said, her mouth struggling into a smile again.

Alia thought her shame might choke her. How poorly she'd judged Imorelle's feelings. How poorly she'd judged her honor. Alia was further shamed to think that if their places were switched, she might not have sought Imorelle out to wish her good luck. "And good luck to you, as well," Alia said, meaning it more than she ever had before.

Imorelle replied in a breaking voice, "My thanks."

Kay and Alia took their leave quietly, letting Imorelle sit alone with her distress. As they left, they didn't run as swiftly as before. "Do you think she'll win an invitation?" asked Alia.

"She should," said Kay. "She's a strong fighter. And she wants to be a warrior woman more than anything else. What would happen to her if she was stuck in an apron?"

"I don't know." Alia shuddered, remembering a girl a few springs back who had wanted very much to join the keentens but wasn't fast enough or strong enough. One morn, after the girl had failed to win an invitation into the Keenten House, she had walked off. No one had ever seen her again. "Maybe Imorelle wouldn't be such a bad sister."

"I've told you that over and over," Kay said.

The girls' excitement returned as they crossed the bridge and then raced up the hill to the Sacred House. An apprentice let them into the Great Hall. They passed through the candlelight and shadows and silently slipped in among the already waiting warrior women. Several keentens leaned over to whisper a greeting. Alia whispered back to them, their familiarity warming her more quickly than the room's roaring fire.

Divin Ospar came into the hall and welcomed them. Then he said, "I want something important from you all."

Alia cast a quick glance at the keentens around her and Kay. Their fierce, glorious faces were turned toward the Divin, waiting and ready for anything he might request of them. Standing elbow to elbow with the warrior women, Alia turned to him as well, sure the glow of her happiness was bursting through her skin.

The Divin rubbed his chin, his many rings flashing in the candlelight. "I'm waiting on Master Nest's thoughts as to what to do with our prisoners. But it would help me to know more of these children. Watch them. Listen to what they say. Anything you can tell me will be important." He looked at Kay and Alia and added, "You two will see them twice each day. Keep your ears wide open and come to me with all you learn."

Kay gave a brisk nod, and Alia said, "We will."

"These eager young things will bring you something," said a keenten named Lara.

And Jen added, "They know better now than to keep important news to themselves." Laughter broke out all around Alia and Kay, and Alia's face felt hot. Then Lara reached over and clapped Alia on the arm, as the warrior women always did with each other when they were jesting and teasing. Alia began to smile, then joined in the ringing laughter like one of the sisters.

Leading the boy back from Raven Wood, Alia had assumed he was clumsy or purposely trying to slow their journey. In the days after meeting with the Divin, she changed her mind. When the boy stood, he put little weight on his right foot. When he walked, he moved like an oversized collup—reluctant and awkward. "What troubles your foot?" Alia often asked him.

"Nothing," he would snap.

"Why would the boy pretend nothing's wrong with his foot?" she asked Kay one morn as they went to the prison. "He has to be hiding something in his boots, something he doesn't want us to see."

"I've been thinking the same thing. He—" Kay broke off, staring at something down near the Smithy. "Tana." Kay spat out the name.

Alia followed Kay's stare. They were on the paths that ran behind the artisans' houses, so they could clearly see the Smithy's back door. Near it was Tana and one of the Smith's apprentices, Marcus Speare. They were standing very close. Very, very close. Alia gaped. "What's she doing?"

Kay looked as if she had tasted something too sour. "You haven't heard? Her father caught her kissing Marcus in the barn and when he yelled at her, she yelled back that she was in love with him. She said Marcus had asked her to marry him. And she said that she'd told him yes."

Alia stopped dead in the path. "Tana?" She remembered how oddly Tana had spoken the other morn outside the Herb House, but this wasn't the kind of explanation she'd expected.

"She says she wasn't ever sure she wanted to join the keentens." Kay's voice was thick with disgust.

"But if the keentens chose her, she could leave the sisterhood later to marry—like your mam did. If she marries now, she can never be a keenten," said Alia, stunned.

Kay tossed her braid over her shoulder. "She says she doesn't care. All she wants to do now is idle around with Marcus, even though they can't marry until she's seen sixteen springs."

"She won't be a sister," said Alia, still shocked.

"Good riddance," said Kay. "I want no warrior sisters who talk of nothing but boys—my blood sisters are bad enough."

Alia agreed, but she couldn't stop staring at Tana. To have fought all these moons for the keentens' attention, and won some praise now and again, then to drop the struggle—how could Tana do such a thing? Once spring came, she wouldn't fight or run the forests; she would be a farm woman, always in an apron. And she had become one of those girls who tied herself to the apron purposely. What could anyone say to a girl like that?

"Come on," Kay said, pulling at her arm. "Forget Tana. We have more important things to think of. Like the boy, and how to find out what he's hiding in his boot."

Alia took one last long look at Tana and Marcus standing so close, the way her sister, Sarian, and Eesa Fairson used to stand when they'd been courting. Alia didn't understand why Tana had changed so suddenly, as suddenly as Sarian had one day seemed to change. But Kay was right, they had more important things to think of. She didn't call out a greeting to Tana before starting toward the Prisoner House, and neither did Kay.

The girls walked slowly so they could scheme

of ways to get the boy to take off his boot. He never wanted to do anything they asked. But there was surely a way to make him, if only they were clever enough to find it.

By the time they entered the prison's dingy hallway, they had struck upon a plan. Kay unlocked and opened the door. Alia went through the doorway, her fingers crossed for good luck. The slop bucket stank, but she strode forward without hesitating. She stopped by the boy.

"So, spies," said Kay, "did you discover anything new last night about Trantian rats?"

Alia hid a grimace. Kay couldn't let a day go by without speaking of the rats—their narrow, greedy faces, their hunger, their scrabbling feet in the dark. Alia stared hard at Kay. They had no time for such games.

Kay seemed to catch the hint. She strolled across the uneven floor and stood under the one lit lantern so the Beechians could see her clearly, as she and Alia had planned.

Alia said, "We have your porridge and bread. Do you want it?"

Neither Beechian answered. They usually didn't. They were used to Kay offering food, then pulling it away several times before she fed them. The girl folded her arms across her chest. The boy examined the creases in his boot. Alia looked for bumps around the boy's ankles or anything else that would give her a hint of what he was hiding. She saw nothing.

"I don't think they're hungry," said Kay. She took the lid off the porridge pot. Steam rose around her face. "Too bad. It smells delicious."

"Maybe we should take it and leave," said Alia, offering her bluff.

"Or we could stand here and eat it for them," Kay said. She dipped her finger into the pot then stuck it into her mouth and slurped.

Alia looked at Kay with irritation. More taunting was not part of the plan. Kay was supposed to be suggesting a trade: food for the boy's boots.

The girl studied the shadowed ceiling, but the boy leaned toward Kay and the porridge pot, unable to stop himself. Alia hid a spark of excitement. Perhaps Kay's persistent taunting would do a service, for once. If the boy's hunger was sharp, he might be more willing to trade. If, however, he refused, Alia wasn't sure what she would do. To truly starve the prisoners would be dishonorable. And she didn't wish to go running to the keentens for help in prying the boot from the boy. The Rina had made it clear that the Beechians were her and Kay's responsibility.

"Boy, take off your boots and show us what's in them. Then we'll give you your morn meal," said Alia.

"What?" the boy cried. At first Alia thought he

was angry, but as two scarlet spots stained his cheeks, she realized he was embarrassed. Confused, she looked to Kay.

"We want to see what you're hiding in your boot," said Kay to the boy, ignoring his embarrassment.

The girl's eyes grew wide. "In his boots?" she asked haltingly. "What do you think is . . . in his boots?"

Despite her confusion, Alia said, "We don't know, but we want to see. We think it must be something important, since he won't even admit he limps."

The boy's oversized hands took up the flute he still wore at his waist. He had never played it, only held it close when Alia and Kay were near, as if he thought they might snatch it from him. Now he gripped it tight, not saying a word.

The girl's thin mouth, surprisingly, began to smile. "I guess asking a man to take off his boots doesn't mean the same thing here as it does in our village."

"And what does it mean?" Kay challenged.

"Girls usually say something like it when they're flirting," the girl said. She smiled wryly at Alia. "It's an invitation made only when a girl seriously considers a suitor."

Alia felt the blood rushing to her face, but she met the girl's smile without flinching. "We don't invite anyone to anything that way here. But your stupid custom does mean that you'd hide something in your boy's boots—because, of course, no one would ask him to take them off," she said.

The girl's smile disappeared. The boy snorted.

The girl said, "We won't take off his boots until you bring a healer."

"No," said the boy sitting straight.

"Yes," the girl insisted, her voice quiet but determined. The boy shook his head.

"A healer," Kay said, her displeasure unmistakable. Kay liked healers even less than Alia did. She thought them gossipy and feather-headed and slow-thinking. Like everyone in her family, she went to the Herb House only when in dire need. "Why a healer?"

"He's hurt," said the girl.

"I think you're lying," said Kay. "Or he'd be asking for a healer himself."

Alia considered the girl's request. It would make no difference either way. If the Beechians were lying, the healer would be one more witness to it. If they were telling the truth, she or Kay would have to fetch a healer anyway.

She whispered to Kay, "We can stand a healer for a few moments to see his boots."

"You can, maybe," Kay whispered back.

"Do you really want to bargain with them all

the morn over something so silly as fetching a healer?" Alia asked.

Kay muttered the worst curse she knew, but shook her head. She said to the girl, "You'll get your healer, but only if we get to look at the boots."

"The healer first," said the girl.

Kay set the food down outside the cell. "I'll give this to you when we have the boots in our hands," she said. Then she grabbed the slop bucket to be dumped on the way and left for the Herb House.

Alia waited in the cell. The Beechians' easy agreement to the trade made her suspicious. She watched them closely, though she didn't like to look at the boy. The thought that she had inadvertently said something that he considered flirtatious made her skin creep.

Alia almost wished she hadn't argued for fetching a healer when she saw who came with Kay: Mari. Mari gave Alia a warm smile, which Alia acknowledged with a nod but didn't answer. The memory of her last unpleasant visit to the Herb House still rankled.

The healer knelt near the Beechians and tucked her hands into the sleeves of her auburn robe. She cast a glance at the food, which sat under the light outside the cell.

"Did you eat this morn?" Mari asked the girl.

"Their food isn't why we brought you here," Kay said, on the border of rudeness.

"But they eat in the morn?" Mari asked politely, as if Kay's sharpness had not been intended for her.

"Of course," answered Kay. "Why do you think we're here?"

"But the food is sitting outside the cell," said Mari.

In a tone that dared Mari to criticize, Alia said, "We want to see what the boy's hiding in his boots. When he shows us, he can have his food."

The healer gave Alia a long, unblinking stare. Alia could tell Mari thought little of the plan, though she said nothing against it. *Still the coward,* Alia wanted to say.

"Let's see the foot," Mari said to the boy.

The boy shrugged away from the healer's touch and said, "Nothing's wrong with me."

"I see," said Mari. "You've been captured and imprisoned without losing a button. Not even a hair on your head is out of place."

The boy glared at Mari. Alia saw a smile twitch the Beechian girl's mouth. Then it disappeared as if it had never existed. It would figure that Beechians and healers shared the same dreadful sense of humor.

"We've other things to do," said Kay, her foot tapping the earthen floor with impatience.

Kay's words had no effect on Mari. The healer

took the time to tuck escaping curls back into her white veil, then said to the boy, "I hear you have a limp."

The boy shifted, pulling his feet underneath him. He began tracing the carvings on his flute.

"Take off the boots," said the girl.

The boy turned to the girl in protest, but something in her rigid, stern face stopped him. He scowled. Then slowly he loosened his laces. Kay's foot stopped tapping against the floor. Alia tilted her head to better see the boy's feet.

As the boy started to pull off his right boot, his face contorted. Alia's brows knitted: something was truly wrong with him. The boy breathed unsteadily as the boot began to slide off. The girl reached out to help him, but he gave her a ferocious frown. She sat back with her hands on her knees.

The boy tried again. Sweat was beading on his forehead. He looked as if he were about to faint. Alia stepped forward to catch him if he should fall.

The boot finally popped off the foot, and a sharp cry of pain broke from the boy. He leaned against the wall behind him. Mari offered her help, but he shook his head. Wearily, he sat up and pulled off the other boot. Even after he had finished, pain lines lingered around his mouth. A fetid stench filled the cell. Alia stared at the rag-wrapped feet, trying to imagine what was hidden underneath the dirty strips of cloth.

Mari asked, "May I?" and gestured to the rags. The boy hesitated, then nodded. Mari gently pulled away the wrappings. As the last rag slid to the floor, Alia sucked in air through her teeth.

Both feet were covered with broken blisters. Mari took the right foot in her hands. Alia walked closer so she could look over the healer's shoulder. She winced as Mari examined a cut that stretched from toes to arch. Most likely, that foot had hurt all the way from Raven Wood, but the Beechian boy had not said a word.

Mari put down the foot, then hunched over her sack. She began pulling out vials. Squinting, she held them before the lantern's sputtering glow.

Alia picked up the boots. She gave one to Kay, then turned her attention to the one she held. Its trengdeer hide was so worn, Alia imagined it had provided little warmth. The wooden sole was thin and, in places, cracked. Nothing was in the boot but bits of stinking rag, which she avoided touching. Alia glanced at Kay.

Kay shook her head. "Nothing."

"It's a wonder he made it here on those feet," Alia said, with a grudging respect.

"It's his own fault," said Kay. "No one asked him to leave Beech. They're still hiding something. I know it."

"We'll find it." Alia said, absently, her thoughts still on the boy and his long, painful trek.

Mari wiped at the dirty feet with a cloth soaked in something, exposing raw blisters to the cell's dim light. The cut on the boy's foot oozed blood. Alia tossed the useless boot by the Beechians' pallets. The boy had no wool foot wrappings or sturdy boots, and the only fire was in the guard's front room, leaving the cell cold. Alia considered what she and Kay should do so their prisoner's feet wouldn't freeze.

Kay handed the Beechians the meal things as Mari said, "I'll fetch some clean rags, at the least. Maybe in the next days I'll be able to find a pair of boots."

At the mention of rags, Alia remembered the mending pile at home that Mam had made for her. It was stacked in an overflowing basket, with tunic sleeves straying out the sides and foot wrappings piled high on top.

"I've been mending foot wrappings at home. Some of them are too worn for anything but the rag pile," Alia said. "I'll bring those for him."

Mari nodded at her, but Kay stared as if Alia were speaking gibberish. "Why? The healer's rags aren't good enough, you think?"

"It's cold in here," Alia said. "And my family has no need for them." She hated how her voice had gone higher and louder, as if she needed to defend herself.

Kay scoffed, "Would they have done the same for your brothers?"

Alia's temper flared. "It doesn't matter what Beechians did to my brothers. These two are our responsibility, and we need to keep them healthy, even if they are only going to be executed."

The word "executed" hung for a moment in the cell, surrounded on all sides by silence. Kay's eyes slid sideways, to the Beechians, then snapped back to Alia. Mari, the boy, and the girl all sat as if frozen. Then each turned away. Mari bent over her work. The girl looked to her food. The boy turned toward the wall, his dark hair hiding his face. Shame made Alia's skin feel too tight. Throwing such a death in the Beechians' faces was no honorable proof of strength. She wished the earthen floor would crack open and swallow her.

"They'll be healthy, with or without your rags," Kay said, her tone offhand, as if Alia had mentioned nothing about executions.

"I'll bring them this eve," Alia said curtly.

Kay's lips tightened, growing thin and pale with anger. No one else said a word.

Seven

Alia and Kay walked through the village toward the Stables, saying nothing to anyone else or to each other. Alia rushed along in quick, angry strides. Kay's pace was just as fast. Neither girl let the other get ahead of her.

At the Stables' door, they both stopped and stared at each other. Alia took a deep breath before saying anything; speaking without thinking had brought her enough pain this morn. Kay, though, broke the silence immediately. "Why do you insist on helping the boy? The keentens won't like it. It makes us look weak. And your rags could go to a better use."

Kay's tone was fierce—but her fingers worried the edge of her cloak. Back and forth, back and forth; the thumb rubbed loose a bit of embroidery, and Kay didn't even seem to notice. Shaken, Alia didn't answer. Kay was truly troubled.

Doubt gripped Alia. Maybe Mari would be

able to bring enough rags. Then if she brought rags as well, the boy might end up with many. And she'd have given him more than he needed when other villagers could use them, like old Widow Glen and her simpleminded son, or Karrine Stilter, who was raising all her small brothers and sisters alone. The keentens would see all this and think her too easily swayed by the enemy children, a poor guard, weak. As Kay feared. Alia's belly squeezed. Why could she do nothing right this day?

"I was wrong," Alia said. "I won't add to the rags Mari will bring."

Kay's hands dropped, hanging loose and easy at her sides. "Good. I'm glad you've found your wits."

Alia flushed. "I wish I'd found them earlier."

"I couldn't believe it when you spoke of the execution." Kay grinned at her. "It's nice to know I'm not the only one who becomes an idiot when I'm angry."

They cleaned the Stables quickly, Kay's good humor cheering Alia. Joking and gossiping, they went back through the village but stopped when they saw a crowd gathered before the Inn. "My mam told me to hurry home," said Kay, taking a step toward the crowd.

"Mine, too," said Alia. "She hates to miss news from the village, though."

Kay laughed. "Mine, too. It's our duty, then, to find out what's happening over there." They ran to get a better look.

The crowd was pressed tightly together, looking at something. "What's going on?" Alia asked the Trader's wife.

The woman adjusted the little boy she held on her hip. Both she and the boy looked as if they'd seen a horde of Beechians. "An absolute horror. A wild dog fought Imorelle, the Weaver's daughter."

Not waiting to hear more, Kay and Alia pushed to the front of the crowd. Imorelle and her father stood before everyone. Imorelle's cheek had a large ragged gash, and she cradled one arm with the other. Her face was drawn and haggard, but she was wearing a proud smile.

"Make way. Make way," Imorelle's father said gruffly. "I need to get her to the healers."

Alia was desperate to hear what had happened, but she stepped aside to let them pass. Instead, though, Jen came through the crowd and filled the gap between Alia and Kay. "What's happened?"

"A wild dog went after our boy, the baby," the father answered. "Imorelle fought it off. It gave me a turn, seeing it jump at her." Alia had never seen a big man shake before. It made her shudder.

Jen went to Imorelle, gently examining the

gash and the arm. "I had no time to call for help," Imorelle explained, grimacing at Jen's touch. "It would have killed Sten."

"We should send out hunters if you wounded it," Jen said. "Put it out of its misery."

"It's dead," said Imorelle with satisfaction.

"Is it?" asked Jen. She gave her a slow, approving nod. "You did the job right, then. After you let the healers tend to you, come see me in the Keenten House."

Murmurs went through the crowd and Kay whispered, "She's done it."

Alia nodded, watching Imorelle smile her most triumphant, glory-bright smile. Imorelle would be a sister. Alia was glad—mostly glad, anyway.

That night, Alia lay in the darkness, eyes wide open. She had heard Mam and Papa take the baby to their small room ages ago, and from behind the curtain that separated her brothers' part of the room from hers came snoring. But the events of the eve haunted her, running through her mind again and again, driving sleep away.

When she and Kay had brought the Beechians their eve meal, she had said her apologies for throwing their execution in their faces. They had said nothing, which she had expected, so she had gone on with the chores—giving them their food, cleaning out the slop bucket. All had seemed to go smoothly.

Then, as Alia bent to pick up the empty stew pot, she had noticed the boy's feet. They had been deftly wrapped, but in few rags. Gaps revealed patches of raw skin. Beside his sleeping pallet had been a small stack of extra rags. A very small stack.

"Is the healer coming later with something for his feet?" Alia had asked the girl.

The girl had shrugged. "She said she'd try but that it would be hard to find boots or such in the winter."

"Of course," Alia had said, knowing this was true. She had stared at the feet, a bad feeling in her belly.

Then she had glanced at Kay, who was standing by the cell's door, her hand on the latch, her face smooth and unconcerned. "Are you ready to leave?" asked Kay.

"Yes," Alia had said. She had turned her back on the prisoners and walked away.

But Alia's belly still hurt. *Always act with honor, even with an enemy,* her elder brothers had always told her. *Especially with an enemy.* Alia thought of the boy's half-bare feet in the prison's chill, and her cheeks burned. A true warrior acted with honor, always. A true warrior stood her ground. She had done neither.

She pushed herself up so she was sitting against the wall. Instead of standing her ground, she had followed Kay's lead—because Kay seemed so surefooted. But Kay was stumbling, too. She wished to keep rags from the boy, though he needed them. She taunted the prisoners ceaselessly. Back in the wood, she had wanted to fight the boy, though there was no need and he clearly wasn't her equal as a fighter. What would the keentens say if they knew these things? Alia stared at the patch of moonlight spilling across the floor, feeling sick.

They were so close to earning an invitation from the warrior women, but they were both acting without thinking. Eagerness was making them lose their heads. She swallowed hard. It would be so awful if they lost the keentens' favor now. She had to talk to Kay. She wished she could run to her friend this very moment, but night was still thick. The morn seemed a long way off, too long.

Alia finally dropped into a restless sleep and woke after everyone else had risen. Mam clucked over her and remarked on her bad color, then brought out the onion-garlic syrup, a foul-tasting remedy that she swore cured most ills. To prove she wasn't ailing, Alia ate an extra portion of bread and porridge, then helped with the dishes without being asked. She took up bread for the prisoners, and a sack of rags as well, and tried to slip out the door unseen. Mam caught her anyway.

"Drink up," Mam insisted.

"I'm late," Alia said.

Mam crossed her arms, blocking her path to the door.

"Drink up," Temmethy repeated, his round face full of feigned concern.

Alia scowled, but choked down the concoction while Temmethy snickered behind one hand. She surreptitiously cuffed the back of his head as she made her escape.

As Alia hurried along the paths, winter's beauty smoothed some of the sharper edges off her worries. The light was a shade of blue-gray found only in winter, and the snow glistened under it like a blanket of clustered stars. The sight of the perfect starry snow made Alia run fast and strong, though she'd slept so little the night before.

As Alia neared the village's edge, Kay called her name and dashed up from the Inn, where she and her papa brought jams and dried fruits in the morns. She put her arm around Alia's shoulder, not seeming to notice the sack. Before Alia could mention it, Kay said, "You smell."

Alia tried to think what she meant, then remembered Mam's remedy. She rolled her eyes as she said, "Mam's onion-garlic syrup cures everything."

"Ugh. I'd rather be sick than drink that nastiness," said Kay. "Do you still have a tongue?"

"Yes, but my breath stinks," Alia answered. She turned quickly, before her friend could escape, and blew, aiming at Kay's nose.

"Stay back!" shouted Kay. She started to run down the Road, weaving past two grand mams with baskets on their arms, and Tana walking with Marcus. With her cape billowing around her and her bulky boots and snow walkers, she looked like an odd web-footed monster.

Alia laughed until it was hard to breathe. Everything suddenly seemed easy to set right. She would speak with Kay this day, as soon as they were alone in the Stables with no one to hear them but the horses. No one would know of their blunders but themselves. She began to chase Kay to the Prisoner House, her laughter trailing behind her.

They stood outside the prison until they had tamed their giggling. Then they went in, fetched the cell's key from Kerrin, the brawny keenten guard, and headed to the back of the prison.

Alia followed Kay into the cell and immediately saw something was wrong. The boy sat near the girl, watching over her. The girl was crunched up on her sleeping mat. One arm was pulled close to her chest, while the other was flung over her brow. Alia studied the two of them warily.

"Time to break your fast," said Kay. "Get your backside up."

"Just leave her be," said the boy. He unfolded himself and stood, leaning on his better foot. It was so ludicrous that he'd challenge Kay when she could clearly knock him over with little effort at all, Alia almost laughed. She was stopped by the ferocity and fear on his face. She looked back to the girl.

Kay handed the boy the bowl of porridge but otherwise disregarded him. She poked the girl's leg with her boot. "Get up," she said.

The girl moved her arm and squinted through the lantern glow. Her cream-colored hair was snarled. Her skin, normally golden brown, was tinged gray like a cloth that has spent the night soaking in dirty dishwater.

Alia passed the bread and the sack of old foot wrappings to the boy, then approached his companion, intending get a closer look. Before she could sit, the boy grabbed her wrist.

"Stay away," Kay said. She yanked the boy back, and he tottered before steadying himself.

"I want to know what she's doing," he said, shrugging off Kay's grip. Kay's menacing stare kept him still but didn't frighten away his scowl.

"Looking at your girl," said Kay shortly, as Alia sat on the girl's sleeping mat.

Alia held up her hands. "Look, no hidden

knives," she said to the boy. His scowl didn't lessen. Alia turned to the girl, ignoring him.

The girl had no strange spots or sores that Alia could see. She laid her hand on the girl's forehead, as Mam did with anyone in the household who was ill. She felt no fever, but something was not right. The muscles around the girl's forehead and neck were tight and knotted.

The girl opened her eyes. They were dull and faded and full of misery. Alia snatched back her hand and rose. The girl didn't need her head felt for fever; she needed someone who knew how to help her.

Kay came closer. "I know what you're trying to do," she said to the girl, as if Alia weren't standing near as well. "Get off the mat."

"Go away," the girl whispered.

Kay squatted, her face less than a hand's width from the girl's face. The boy moved closer to them.

"Kay—" Alia started.

Kay interrupted her. "Listen," she said to the girl, her tone sharp.

"No, your voice is too loud," moaned the girl. She curled into a ball, her hands pressed over her ears.

Alia gave Kay an irritated stare, but Kay didn't notice her. Instead, she sat back on her haunches, her look roaming over the girl. Before Alia could speak again, Kay laughed, shaking her head. "How long is your girl planning on doing this?" she asked the boy.

The boy put his hand protectively on the girl's shoulder. He answered, "Take back the food. When she's like this, she can't eat."

Kay laughed again. She shrugged and picked up the pot. "Fine. Play your game, but keep the bread. I'll have no one say I neglected to feed you," she said, then stood and left them.

The boy refolded himself, his long arms wrapped around his knees. Alia turned her back on him and the girl, hating to have to take their side against her friend. Then she stalked out of the cell.

Outside the Prisoner House, she almost bumped into Kay, who stood in the middle of the path. Kay glared at Alia. "What were you doing in there? You rushed over to that girl. You touched her, even. What if she had grabbed you?"

Alia scoffed. "She couldn't have attacked me. She's obviously hurting."

"Hurting," Kay said, her voice thick with contempt. "Hurting? She's trying to deceive us. They're taking the coward's way, pleading for sympathy so we won't execute them. It's disgusting. Open your eyes."

Alia fought to keep her voice low and steady. "My eyes are open, and I think we should fetch a healer."

Kay leaned close. "You *what?*"

Kay was so certain she was right; Alia couldn't stand it. "She's ill!" Alia yelled.

"She's fooled you. She's making an ass of you," Kay sneered.

Alia's cheeks stung as if Kay had slapped her. "You're the ass. You're failing your responsibility." Alia pointed her finger in Kay's face. "You're failing the keentens' test."

Kay stepped back, her eyes full of surprise and hurt. Then her expression hardened. "*I'm* failing the keentens' test? Take a good look at yourself, Alia Cateson." She walked away, down the path. Turning onto the Road, she joined the other bundled figures who strolled or loitered or hurried to their destinations. She didn't once glance behind her.

Alia watched, her hands clenched tight. Kay disappeared. Leaving the girl sick in the cell. Leaving Alia to take care of everything.

"Fine," Alia muttered ferociously. She turned and reentered the Prisoner House.

Kerrin, the guard, looked up from a piece of wood she was whittling. "Yes?" she asked.

"I'm going to the Herb House to fetch a healer. The girl is sick," said Alia.

Kerrin nodded, though her face showed no expression. "As you think best. They're your responsibility," she said, then looked back down at her knife and her wood.

Suddenly uncertain, Alia watched the knife scrape the wood. The keenten's answer had shown no approval. Alia could hear Kay's voice in her head, saying, *You see? The girl is making an ass of you.*

But Kerrin had shown no disapproval, either. Warrior women used the healers when they had to, and the Beechian girl needed healing. Kay was the ass. And Alia wouldn't let Kay's poor judgment rule her any longer.

When Alia reached the Herb House, she knocked impatiently on the door. No one answered her knock, so she let herself in. The common room was empty. She crossed to the kitchen. Empty. She hurried on, vexed not to find someone immediately. It was bad enough that she had had to come alone; she shouldn't have to spend the entire morn searching for a healer.

She pulled open the herbarium door. Thick, moist air engulfed her. It was as if she had walked into summer's refuge. Her irritation melted away as the room's sweet scent filled her nose, her hair, her skin. Looking down the rows of plants, Alia saw Mari at a table near the fire, her hands busy with a jumble of earth, plants, and pots. Dirt was smudged across the side of the healer's face. She didn't notice Alia.

"Mari?" Alia said.

Mari looked up. When she saw it was Alia,

she gave neither a greeting nor a smile, saying only, "Yes?"

Alia tilted up her chin, not liking the healer's chill. Worse, she knew she deserved it. Yestermorn's ill-said words suddenly seemed all the more awful because Mari had witnessed them.

"I came because of the Beechians," Alia said. Mari nodded, but said nothing. Alia continued. "The girl is ailing. Her head hurts so badly, she won't eat."

Mari asked, "Her head hurts from sickness or something else?"

Alia did not grasp the healer's meaning at first. Then the words' significance stabbed at her. "Because of an illness, of course," she snapped. "She's a prisoner. No one would hurt her, unless she attacked first."

"Is she feverish? Vomiting?" Mari asked.

When Alia answered no, Mari said, "Still, it could be serious. I suppose these little things will have to wait." Her hand brushed some bell-shaped flowers that werc too big for the pots that now held them. Then she looked up at Alia. "Thank you for coming," she said with a cool politeness.

Mari's tone brought back Alia's flush of shame. Instead of leaving, she said, "Yestermorn I said something awful. And cruel. I won't do it again."

Mari's lips parted with surprise. Then a slow smile spread across her face.

"I'm glad to hear you admit it," she said. "I should have known you would. You always were decent."

"You always thought me decent?" Alia asked, as Mari pushed up her sleeves and washed her hands in a bucket.

Mari dried her forearms and gestured for Alia to follow her into the common room. "Yes. I remember you playing with our other cousins. You were strong, but not cruel."

Alia was amazed that the healer remembered such things of her. Mari had entered the Herb House when Alia had seen only eight springs.

"Now, tell me about Kyrra," Mari said as she went to the hooks by the door where the cloaks hung.

"Kyrra?" Alia asked, trying to follow the healer's skittering thoughts.

"The Beechian girl," Mari answered. "Kyrra. And her brother is Rhys, from Dawn Groves," said Mari.

Alia stared at Mari for the measure of a few heartbeats. Intrigued, she asked, "How did you get them to tell you their names and where they're from?"

"I asked them," answered Mari.

Alia gave a loud bark of laughter. Ruefully,

she thought that maybe she and Kay had been more stupid than she had supposed. They had never even considered asking the Beechians straight questions. "What else did you ask?"

Mari dug through a box of hoods and mittens. "This and that. We talked for a bit after you left the prison yestermorn," she said without looking up.

"This and that," Alia repeated. "This and that" didn't sound like someone asking a spy questions. It sounded like a conversation over tea.

Alia watched Mari pull on a cloak and mittens. Mild concern wrinkled the healer's forehead, but she seemed otherwise untroubled. In truth, she acted as if she were stepping out to tend to friends, rather than simply fulfilling a responsibility. A sour taste filled Alia's mouth.

"Didn't the Beechians kill Ewan, the Miller's son, whom you were going to marry?" Alia demanded.

Mari stopped dressing, though one of her hands was still bare. "Yes," she said, her voice snapping like a breaking twig.

"So how can you be nice to them?"

Mari pulled her cloak around her. "Because I want this to end someday," she said, with a passion Alia had never seen in her before. Then she turned and left, slamming the door behind her.

Alia stood alone in the Herb House, staring at

the door but not really seeing it. The Beechians had started the war and continued to drag it on and on. Her people and the entire Divinhood were trying to end the fighting, struggling to crush the rebellion so all the Magus's provinces could have peace. What did Mari mean?

Alia walked slowly out into the snow. Something was strange. Something that involved Mari and the Beechians. She scanned the ground, searching for answers that weren't written there.

The sight of her shadow startled her, and she looked up at the sun. She had been longer in the Herb House than she had intended. Kay was probably halfway done in the Stables by now. Alia quickened her pace, then slowed it again. She had had no help in tending to the problem of the sick girl. Why should she run to help Kay?

When she reached the Stables, Alia removed her snow walkers, then slid open the door of the building. The scent of leather and hay, sweat and manure wrapped around her. She walked by a few inquisitive horse faces, looking for Kay in the middle stalls. Her edginess irritated her. She had done nothing wrong. Kay was the one who should apologize.

The middle stalls were clean, as was most of the rest of the Stables. Alia spotted Kay by the far door, shoveling out the last of the stalls. Relieved, Alia smiled. Left on her own to think, Kay must have changed her mind about the girl needing a healer. She had done Alia's share of the stalls, as well as her own, as a peace offering. Alia winced, thinking of the things she had said to Kay, wishing she could unsay them. She shouldn't have lost her temper—Kay had only needed a little time to admit her mistake.

Offering a warm greeting, Alia grabbed a shovel and joined her friend. Kay straightened. She threw her shovel into the wheelbarrow. "I don't need your help," Kay said coldly, then started down the hallway, alone.

Eight

"What's that supposed to mean?" Alia demanded.

Kay pushed her wheelbarrow to the door of the stall. "I don't need your help, and I don't want it, either."

"You *do* need my help." Alia followed Kay right to the door and leaned against it so Kay would have to face her. She met Kay's furious look with a steady glare. "Without me, the girl would have no help from a healer, and you'd be in trouble with the keentens."

"Without you, I'd be in no trouble. You're the one bringing trouble on to us both." Kay smacked her hand against a thick post. "They want a healer, you fetch a healer. They pretend to be ill, you fetch a healer again. You even brought the boy rags, didn't you? I saw you hand him a sack."

"I did. He needed them. Just as the girl needed a healer. How can you not see that?" Alia spun away in frustration, then turned back to Kay. "What would the keentens say if they knew you'd let the boy's feet freeze? Or that back in the woods, you wanted to untie him and fight him again, even though he was safely caught?"

Kay flushed at Alia's last words but snapped, "Fighting would have been a mistake. But for the rest—the keentens would say nothing. It's you they'd call weak. You run here and there, fetching everything they ask for."

"I fetch them what they need," Alia said, low and fierce. "As any *honorable warrior* would."

"When did you become such a fool?" Kay asked. Then she said very slowly, "It's the boy, isn't it? He does have some height, for a Beechian, and dark hair. Without those eyes, he could almost pass for one of us."

Alia's mouth dropped open. "What?" she whispered.

"There aren't many strong men here to look on because of the war," Kay said, her face full of revulsion. "Maybe he makes your heart race."

Alia heard herself say, "Keentens renounce men."

"Oh?" Kay let her words fly sharp and hard, like arrows. "You still want to be a keenten?"

The words bit into Alia, piercing her to the marrow. She stared at Kay, unable to speak.

Kay went on as if she didn't notice Alia's

silence. "My aunt is ill, and my mam wants help tending her and her brood. We leave this eve for her village and will be gone the next eve as well. The Rina approved of my leaving. She said you'd be fine. I hope the Beechians don't decide their cell isn't comfortable enough. You'd probably let them out to relieve their misery." Kay left, slamming the door behind her.

Alia looked at the door. Never had Kay flung such insults at her before. She realized her nose was running and her throat was tight. She kicked at a stall. She would not cry. Kay certainly was not crying right now.

Alia finished cleaning the Stables, then began to trudge home. All the while, the pain inside was like that of a cut that had festered—hot and sharp and relentless. She couldn't make it stop.

She wanted only to be alone and quiet, but when she reached home, she found Imorelle there. Papa and Imorelle's papa were together in the shed. "They're fixing one thing or another," Mam said with a wave of one hand, which meant she thought that they were trading more gossip than work. Imorelle sat at the table telling of her fight with the wild dog while Alia's younger brothers listened with open mouths. Imorelle was making herself sound like a keenten of old, unfearing, untiring, fighting better than anyone now could truly fight. Alia gave her a brusque greeting, then went to the corner and crouched next to her dreary mountain of mending. Imorelle went on with the grand tale, and a bad taste filled Alia's mouth. Once they both entered the Keenten House, she'd have to hear such stories from Imorelle night and day.

"What does it feel like?" Athon gestured at Imorelle's bandaged face, his thick, square hand tentative.

"It hurts a bit," Imorelle admitted. "Not too bad, though."

"That's enough now. You have work to do," Mam scolded the boys. "Let Imorelle and Alia talk."

"Mam!" Temmothy objected, but her expression stopped him. Grumbling, he and Athon went off to help Papa.

Imorelle came to sit next to Alia. Alia bent over her mending, as if working hard. "Alia, what did you do to Kay?" Imorelle whispered.

Surprised, Alia looked up from her basket. "What do you mean?"

"I've been here all morn, bored stiff. I knew Kay was leaving, so I ran over to wish her well while my papa talked with yours. You must have said something awful to her. She looked as if she'd been crying, and I've never seen Kay cry. She said she didn't know what was wrong with you."

"Nothing. Nothing's wrong with me," Alia answered, thinking of Kay crying. At least Kay was feeling bad, too.

"Well, obviously something's wrong between you. I can help you sort things through." Imorelle sounded sure Alia would beg for her help.

"Thanks, but it's nothing." Alia pretended her mending was so fascinating that she didn't have time to chat. Imorelle didn't catch the hint. She settled herself beside Alia, giving advice on resolving arguments. Blessedly, Papa, the boys, and Imorelle's papa came in and Imorelle had to leave. When they said farewell, Alia could barely hide her relief.

Left alone with her thoughts, she watched her fingers moving but didn't see what was before her. Kay was upset. Did she know she'd been wrong? When they first saw each other, what would they say? Unanswerable questions filled Alia's head, jostling and pushing one another until she accidentally stabbed herself with the sewing needle. She muttered a curse she'd only heard said in the Smithy.

"Are you still ill, Alia? I can fetch some onion-garlic syrup," Mam offered.

"I'm fine," Alia answered quickly. Then she added, "I'm just tired of the Beechians."

"Should be done with 'em soon," said Papa as he handed the boys more tools to grease.

"If the Divin can decide what to do with them," said Mam, shaking her head.

"Execute 'em," said Papa. "Nasty thing, but it has to be done. Spies are spies."

Alia didn't look up, wincing over how she had thrown the Beechians' deaths in their faces. At the two executions she had seen, the keenten or warrior executioners wore dark hoods pulled far forward so no one would recognize them. Killing someone whose hands were tied was nothing to be proud of.

"Well, I won't argue with you, Geoffrey," said Mam. She gestured to Alia with her knit needles. "You know how your father is: once he's facing one direction, there's no turning him around. If I say go east, he goes west. If I say plant seed on the full moon, he plants it on the new moon."

"Grows better on the new moon," said Papa.

Alia almost smiled.

Mam said, "You see? But these spies are still children. Not warriors like Geoffrey Younger and James were." She paused after saying the names, as if letting some hurt pass through her, but the thick grief and tears didn't come. Alia shared a quick look of relief with the boys and Papa while Mam went on. "The Beechians might treat children as grown, but that doesn't mean we should."

Papa pulled out his pipe and placed it between

his teeth. "But they're enemy spies. We can't just let them go free."

Mam answered, "I don't call drudge work freedom. Still, I won't argue. At the least, I think we should ask what they're doing here. But I know it's no use arguing."

Papa grinned around the stem of his pipe. "Sounds to me like you're arguing."

Mam continued, as if Papa hadn't spoken. "I expect you'll get your wish, Geoffrey. From listening to most of those speaking up at the Village Council, you'd think executions are almost as glorious as fighting. Unless the master speaks against it, the Divin will choose to put them to death. No doubt about it."

Alia hunched over her work, her mood darkening. The Beechians might deserve to be executed, but killing in that way held no honor. And in truth, Alia didn't look forward to watching.

When Alia left to return to the prison that eve, a ripple of clouds blotted out the early stars. She stood on the path, away from the house, away from everyone—Mam, Papa, the keentens, the Beechians, Kay. She wished she needn't go anywhere, just stand in silence and watch night swell and grow.

She breathed in cold air and noticed the shadow of the old allam tree beside her. It was gnarled and eerie. For the first time since delivering the prisoners to the keentens, she thought of the eerie blue shadows of Raven Wood and of the strange screams only she had heard. She glanced over her shoulder and saw the wood's dark outline in the distance.

She studied it. She should ask the Divin about the screaming, though the answer, if there was one, didn't seem so important anymore. The wood held wild, inexplicable magic. Magic untamed by the divins or the masters or even the Magus himself. Magic that she, as a keenten, would never truly understand.

The tip of her nose grew cold as she watched the dark stretch of trees. It seemed a long time since she had walked among them. A long time, back before the keentens had treated her like one who might join them. Before she had started fighting with Kay. She shook her head irritably; she had thought enough of Kay this day. She turned back to the path.

She ran to the prison, snow falling around her in large, slow-moving flakes. The village road was mostly empty, so she could run as fast as she wanted past the Inn and the artisans' houses. The day's frustration, anger, and hurt eased a bit, soothed by the eve wind's whispers in her ears. Then she realized it wasn't just the wind that was whispering.

A faint, haunting tune drifted among the snowflakes. The song was familiar but strange, like a friend in a dream who looks nothing like she does in the waking world. For a moment, Alia thought that the mischievous night spirits had emerged for a romp. Or maybe the foxes were playing flutes, trying to charm the rabbits from their holes. Except that the music was coming from the prison.

The keenten guard—it was Lara this night—let her into the light and the song.

"He's been playing since dusk," Lara said, stretching her feet closer to the fire. "It's not half bad."

Alia followed the music down the hallway. Its beauty seemed strange, surrounded by the dirty walls, the chill, and the dim gloom. It was like a piece of the sky trapped in the dark, reeking prison.

Alia unlocked the cell, her ears following the melody's sway. She walked in and saw Kyrra. Alia forgot the music and stared.

The Beechian girl was sitting up, leaning against the wall. Her head was tipped back, and her arms were wrapped around her chest. The expression on her face was full of a weary pain. Alia suddenly remembered it holding another kind of pain, sharp and anguished. Kyrra was the girl whom Alia had seen screaming in sorrow after the fire at the healers' trade meeting.

"You were at the Blessed Groves," Alia said.

The music broke off on an unnatural note.

"You were there?" Kyrra asked.

"I saw you as we left," Alia said. She realized Rhys must have been the boy standing beside Kyrra. "And him, too."

Though Kyrra still looked tired and ill, she straightened and asked, "What else did you see at the groves?"

Alia didn't answer at first. She wanted to know what Kyrra had seen, for any tidbit could be important to the Divin, but sharing too much of what she knew with the Beechians might be a mistake. "Keentens and warriors meeting in the clearing. There was smoke, and everyone ran." She asked, "What did you see?"

Kyrra answered with another question. "You didn't see the hooded men, the men pretending to be healers from the mountains?"

Alia didn't like this reply, for it seemed Kyrra was playing the same game as she was. Again, she spoke with care. "The only men I saw were the warriors who rushed to fight the fire. Did you see the hooded men? Were they Borderland sorcerers?"

"Borderland sorcerers," Rhys said disdainfully.

"Exiles from the Borderlands prowl for goods. These men took no provisions, only killed. We think they were from the Divinhood," Kyrra said.

Alia's throat tightened with revulsion at Kyrra's suggestion. She answered, "What happened was awful. No Divin would have done it." Then she added, in a tone that dared Kyrra to contradict her, "And you're the rebels. If you had stopped fighting, your healers would have been safe."

Rhys stood, his flute clutched in his hands. "Stop fighting? Before the war, most people were always hungry, except those in the Sacred Houses. When I played music for the divins' families and the apprentices, the table scraps were a feast. We won't return to that."

Kyrra put a hand on Rhys's arm, but he didn't stop. "And the Divinhood was killing healers, anyway," he added.

Alia shook her head, dismissing his false words.

Kyrra said in an even tone, "Ask your Divin about the Trials in Beech. Eldresses were taken away for 'overstepping their role.' No one ever saw them again."

"Don't lie to me hoping for sympathy," Alia scoffed.

Kyrra asked, "You doubt me? You can't close your eyes to what happened in the groves. Even sorcerers don't have that kind of magic, only divins. They want to destroy us."

Alia answered, "If the killers weren't Exiles' sorcerers, they were probably some divin's apprentices who were trying to terrify you so you'd lay down your weapons. Unlike you Beechians, some of us want this to end."

Rhys broke in before Kyrra could stop him. "I want this to end. I want a lot of things I can't have. I want to leave this cold, stinking cage."

His voice grew low and rough. "I want our sister back. She was burned in that grove. She was a healer and didn't deserve—" His voice cracked, and he stopped speaking. He turned awkwardly away and leaned against a wall with his back to Alia.

Alia spoke in a rush of outrage. "And I've lost no one? My elder brothers were both killed in a skirmish three winters past. Both dead because of your stupid, selfish war."

She stopped and bit the inside of her cheek. She had let her anger carry the argument far from a place where she could find out anything from the Beechians, and she had let them know too much about her. She stared defiantly at Rhys's thin back. She would not say too much again.

Alia looked down and saw she still held the Beechians' food. She thrust the bread and the stew pot to Kyrra. Then she backed away and crossed her arms.

Kyrra took the pot, saying in a tired voice, "Two brothers is a lot to lose at once."

Alia glanced at Kyrra's face. The girl looked bone weary, as if the conversation had wrung all the strength out of her. Her expression held no hint of insincerity or cruelty.

"Yes," Alia answered, uncomfortable with Kyrra's kindness.

"But you have the groves," said Rhys.

"Groves?" Alia asked warily.

Rhys turned around. "The Groves of the Dead," he said, as if Alia were a bit dim. "For their ashes."

"We bury our dead on our land," Alia said.

"So you have their burial spot," said Rhys, shrugging.

"No, I don't." Alia said the words as if they didn't matter to her in the least. "The fighting was too thick, and the other warriors had to leave my brothers where they lay."

"Oh," said Rhys. He turned the flute over and over in his hands. "I'm sorry."

Alia searched for something to say. "What did you do for your sister?"

Rhys glared down at the flute. "We sprinkled ashes from the Blessed Grove that burned in the Groves of the Dead."

"So her spirit will rest easy, then," said Alia. Unlike the spirits of her brothers. She stared straight ahead, willing the tightening ache in her chest to leave.

Rhys sat by Kyrra and ate a few bites of stew and bread, then left the rest for his sister. Kyrra ate as if she were uncertain of her stomach, sopping small pieces of the bread in the stew until they were soft before chewing them. Alia leaned against the wall, waiting and wishing she were already back in the warmth of her home.

Rhys raised his flute to his lips and began a slow, bittersweet song. Alia didn't listen closely at first. Then the flute's voice lowered and warbled like a lonely bird. It cried out as if hurting. It moaned like the wind. Alia looked at Rhys and listened.

The music made the whole room seem changed. Kyrra looked older and sad and beautiful, like a divin's daughter disguised as a beggar girl in a story. Rhys's fingers were no longer too large or clumsy. They danced over the flute's slender body. Alia felt she, too, was different; all her feelings were close to her skin, instead of hidden away.

The music pushed and pulled at her, trying to drag tears from her, then bubbling in her like laughter. The tones were dark and light, sun and moon, stars and snow and air. They were the deaths in fall and the births in spring and the warm, sweet sunlight of summer. They wove together, singing through Alia with a precious, important meaning, a wordless meaning she could feel but not name.

Alia didn't know how long she had stood listening when the music curled around itself and ended, as softly as a lullaby. Its absence was a loss.

She wiped her face slowly, as if she were weary, not crying. She walked forward to fetch the meal things. As she bent to get the pot from Kyrra, she saw that Rhys was staring at her. Their eyes met, and Alia knew from his look that he knew he had made her cry. She waited for him to say something sharp, something that would wound her. After hearing such music, she had no sharp words in her to fight back.

He didn't, though, only looked quickly away. Alia straightened with the pot in her hands and wondered if she were ill. Though she knew the room was cold, she felt suddenly warm and dizzy. She adjusted her cloak, waiting for her head to clear.

"Do your Trantian musicians know that song?" Rhys asked.

"No. . . . I don't know. . . . I haven't heard many musicians," answered Alia, still trying to find her bearings.

"I suppose I won't find out," he said.

Alia felt a twisting inside. If Rhys was executed, his music would be killed, too. "You may not be executed," she said, her words sounding too loud in the little cell. "The Divin hasn't decided."

"He'll choose execution," said Kyrra.

Alia felt another twisting and said, "We won't know until he hears from the master."

Rhys stood and looked down at her. He was so close she could see that his eyes were speckled like the stones in a sunbathed riverbed. He said, "You've already helped us. You could have let Kyrra suffer this morn, but you fetched a healer. We've no way to thank you, but we need another favor. We need—" He looked back at Kyrra, who sat so still she seemed not to breathe. "I want to know when your divin has decided. I want . . ." He stared steadily at her. "I want to be prepared."

Alia nodded once, thinking of his music and Kyrra's kind words about her brothers. The Beechians deserved that much. She said, "It's only right you should know."

Nine

Alia knew she should speak to the keentens about the Beechians and the Blessed Groves straight away, without waiting to speak to Kay. But she would talk to Kay first, and Kay would hear the hard truth. Taunting, threats, and insults had won no answers from the prisoners; instead, the right questions simply had to be asked. If Kay still thought her a weak fool or lovestruck by the boy, she could find someone else to run with.

Alia had to wait a whole day and night for Kay, though. Her thoughts churned around and around: Kay would apologize, Kay would be angry, Kay would admit she'd been wrong, Kay would hurl more insults. The walls of every place Alia stepped inside were too close, making her churning thoughts crowded, almost unbearable. At the prison, she spoke with Rhys and Kyrra, but they told her nothing new, and she quickly fled the small cell. At home, she couldn't sit still.

The boys avoided her. Mam and Papa scolded her. Even the baby chose other laps for shelter. Finally, Mam sent her outside, saying she could do as she pleased as long as she begged, borrowed, or stole a better temper before she came home.

Alia gladly left the house. She didn't bother strapping on snow walkers. She pushed through the snow's drifts, the heavy dampness pressing against her legs. She moved as fast as she could, leaning into the snow until her legs ached and her head was filled with one thought: the thought of the next step.

Looking only as far as the drifts before her, Alia strode through her farm's farthest fields. The strength it took to move in the snow made her sweat, so she paused to loosen her cloak. She looked up for the first time in what seemed like ages, and almost stepped backward at the sight of Raven Wood.

Orange leaves hung from branches like majestic jewels. Twisted trunks sparkled with ice; melted water must have trickled down them during a warm day, then frozen when the weather cooled. Alia could see glints of orange and gold and yellow even from deep within the wood. Slowly, she walked closer, squinting against the wood's brightness.

Then she stopped and stared, a strong memory

taking hold of her; the memory that had eluded her when she took one last look at the wood on the day she'd captured the Beechians. In one of the Old Tales, a healer had come to a wood in winter, "when ice ran down the trees in rivulets." Bandits had raided the healer's village, and she had run to escape. She had hidden within the wood, and the trees had shrieked and frightened the bandits away.

Woods used to speak. They still did, rarely. A very few had heard them.

Alia slogged toward the wood, her legs no longer weary. When she stood beside a gnarled trunk, she looked up into its branches.

"It was you I heard, wasn't it?" she asked, though she expected no answer. Trees didn't speak with words, just sounds: moans, sighs, whispers, screams. These trees had screamed their displeasure when Kay was caught in her fight blindness. Kay had heard them a little, enough to distract her. But Alia had truly heard them.

Just, she realized suddenly, as she had heard one of the Blessed Groves whispering while it burned—and then had heard its silence. She had not been confused by imaginings that day. She could hear the trees in a way most others couldn't. In a way few had since long ago.

She looked into the secretive shadows, then

up to the towering crown of leaves. "I can hear you," she whispered.

One single leaf dropped from a branch.

Alia stared as the leaf drifted to the snow. Her heart beat a bit faster, for the wood never lost its leaves until late winter. She scanned the wood's edge. No other leaves had fallen, only the one before her.

She looked down at it. Usually, when Raven Wood's leaves fell, they were thin and crisp and brown. This one was still brilliant orange, with golden veins and a golden stem. It sparkled and shone, as if a bit of the sun had dropped to the ground.

Alia pulled off her mittens and picked it up. It was as supple as a piece of finely woven cloth. She laid it in her palm. A warmth flowed into her hand, up to her fingertips, then down her arm and all through her. She looked up at Raven Wood.

"My thanks." Alia felt a fierce surge of pride. Kay's mam had sometimes told her and Kay stories about the time when keentens, and everyone else, could hear the trees. In those times, warrior women traveling in woods were guided by the trees to safe caves for night shelter. Once, when a keenten had been hurt by enemies and wandered through a grove, weak with pain and starving, the trees' sighs had led her to a village. Kay's mam had said, "Our ears have grown duller since then. It's too bad. It would be useful for a keenten to have such aid." And Alia did have such aid. She might not fight as well as Kay, or have Imorelle's strength, but she could hear the trees.

She tucked the leaf into her tunic's inner chest pocket. Through the wool of her shirt, she still could feel its warmth. She looked down at herself, but she looked the same—brown cloak wrapped around brown wool tunic and black wool leggings. Her hair tumbled down to her waist, unruly as always. No one would know by looking at her that she hid something that glowed and shone in an inner pocket. No one would know what she could hear. The power of such secrets made her taste an unusual sweetness in her mouth. She would share these secrets—with Kay, once they mended their friendship, and then with the keentens—but not just yet. For now they would be only hers.

Alia woke early the next morn, the day she would see Kay again. Her belly fluttered unpleasantly. She ignored it and dressed, as if this were any other day.

When she had finished dressing, she started out of her room, then stopped. She needed one more thing. She went back to her sleeping pallet, careful to make no sound that might wake her still sleeping brothers. At her pallet, she knelt and reached under her pillow, half expecting to feel nothing.

The leaf was still there. With a smile, she pulled it out. It was warm and slightly rough, like someone's hand lying against her own. She slowly traced its edge, then tucked it into her tunic's inner pocket. Her secret would be with her, no matter what the day brought.

Since she wasn't hungry, Alia took a heel of bread to gnaw, as well as bread for the Beechians, and left for the prison. She stopped to wait at the old split elm that stood between her farm and Kay's, in case Kay came along. Kay didn't come. Alia ran on.

At the edge of the village, Alia saw ahead of her on the Road a tall, thin girl with a braid—Kay. She wasn't alone, though; she walked with Imorelle. They were shoulder to shoulder, Imorelle talking, Kay bending her head toward the shorter girl. Surprised, Alia slowed. She didn't call out.

Imorelle and Kay walked on. Alia had never seen them talk so, as if they had much to say to each other, as if they had an important secret to discuss. Outrage filled Alia. Kay would not come to meet her but would meet Imorelle and talk over some secret with her? Alia scowled. She hoped Kay stumbled and spilled the pot of porridge she was carrying all over them both.

Then another thought made Alia go very still, the thought that they were talking of her and her fight with Kay. Even though Alia hadn't wanted Imorelle to do anything about the argument, Imorelle would surely still try and "help" so she could claim the honor of making things right. Kay might not mind accepting such "help," but Alia wanted none of it. Not one drop. "Kay! Imorelle!" Alia yelled. The other girls didn't seem to hear her.

Alia began to run to them, but just then Imorelle left Kay, heading up the path toward the Loom House. Alia cursed herself for waiting so long. Now she couldn't tell Imorelle to keep her nose out of other people's troubles. "Kay!" she yelled again.

Kay stopped and turned. Alia ran up. Though Kay's expression was unreadable, Alia was hit by the stark memory of the twist of her mouth, the disgust, the accusation that Alia cared for the Beechian boy. Pain and anger made a hard knot in her throat. She willed her face to hold no hint of what was inside her. Kay was not the only one who could hide away what she felt.

"We should be getting to the prison," said Kay. No greeting. No news of her trip. No apology.

"We should," Alia answered and started walking so fast that Kay fell behind her. She should say something. She should tell of the Beechians. But the knot in her throat would let nothing out.

Alia reached the prison door. From behind her, Kay said, "Wait, Alia. I should say something. About what I said. About you and the boy."

Alia stopped and turned, everything in her tensed. Kay said, "My apologies. It was an awful thing to say."

The knot in Alia's throat unraveled. She swallowed hard. "It was. Apologies accepted. And what of the rest—the boy's feet, and the healer for the girl?"

Kay stared, her eyes like hard black stones. "I thought you'd give apologies for those."

Alia's throat squeezed. She forced words through it. "I'm not wrong about those, Kay."

Kay's chin jutted forward. Alia realized it had been hard for Kay to apologize, but she'd done it because she'd expected an apology in return. Too bad for her. Alia had nothing to apologize for.

Kay pushed past Alia without a word and went into the prison. Alia didn't want to follow at Kay's heels. She would rather wait out in the chill air for Kay's return. Then they would settle this, once and for all.

She had no choice, though; the keenten guard would be watching for her. With heavy feet, she walked into the prison, walked by the guard, walked down the hallway to the cell.

Kay didn't acknowledge her. Rhys and Kyrra looked mistrustful and sullen; gone was the wary courtesy she had seen in them during Kay's absence. Alia passed them the loaf of bread. She stepped back and leaned against the cold wall, saying nothing to anyone. She would do only what she had to, nothing more.

"Our invalid is up," Kay said, as if "invalid" were a taunt. She thrust the porridge pot at Kyrra, who took it and started to eat.

"She's stronger," Alia answered, her tone as cold as the wall at her back.

Kay's laughter was unkind. "So strong you'd hardly believe she'd been ill."

"I guess you'd have had to be here in the last days to know for sure," said Alia, shortly. "But you weren't."

"I didn't have to be here." Kay studied the eating Beechians. "I do know for sure."

The flickering light cast shadows around Kay. They framed her face, which glowed with severity, pride, and strength. She looked like one of the magic visions the Divin wove of air and fire for all to see, a lithe, fierce warrior woman from long past, who protected all from harm.

But Kay was harming, not protecting, no matter how she appeared or what she believed. And the Beechians were witness to it. Alia looked away from Kay, down at the toes of her boots, over at the cell's dark corners. She felt chilled. How could Kay be so sure, and so wrong?

Kay spoke into the silence. "The village I visited was near the border. One of its war parties had just arrived home with a whole village of Beechian prisoners. We feasted to celebrate their success."

Rhys stopped eating, though he had taken few mouthfuls. He picked at the edges of his bread. Kyrra hesitated, then continued eating as if Kay were speaking of trivial things.

Alia knew Kay had intentionally not named the village so Rhys and Kyrra would fear for their family and friends. Alia asked, "What was the village called?" The prisoners looked up. Kyrra's face held no expression, but Rhys looked as if he were steeling himself for the worst kind of news.

"I don't really remember," Kay said, shrugging. Alia clenched her hands into fists. As soon as she and Kay were alone, she would bring an end to this.

An unpleasant silence filled the cell. Kay went to the outhouse to dump the slop bucket. Alia didn't offer her help. No one spoke again.

When the Beechians had finished, Alia and Kay left the prison, one behind the other, as if they had never met before. Kay walked fast and stared straight ahead. Alia held her pace steady, refusing to chase after Kay. She didn't want to argue in the Road, where the Divin's daughters were walking and the Smith's son and the Trader stood gossiping. The distance between the two girls grew.

Alia didn't go straight into the Stables after Kay. She stood with her hand on the latch and went over what she would say. Her own nervousness disgusted her. She had right on her side. Kay should be the nervous one. She yanked open the door and stepped inside.

Kay was already shoveling. Alia walked forward. She felt as if she were pushing against Kay's silence. The silence seemed to push back. It wanted her to leave. She shoved at it.

Outside the stall next to Kay's, Alia stopped. Kay didn't look up.

"The Beechians talked a good deal while you were gone," Alia said.

Kay didn't stop her work. "So?"

"You know, Mari learned their names and where they came from, simply by asking. Then I recognized the girl: as we left the healers' trade meeting, I saw her by the mounts with the boy. So I asked them if they were at the trade meeting, just like that—no threats, nothing." To finally be able to show Kay the truth made her feel lighter. She let the words continue to pour from her. "They admitted they were there, at the Blessed Groves, during the burning. I asked, and they told me."

Kay straightened, looking thoroughly astonished. Then she began to laugh so loudly one of the mares snorted in disapproval. "They were at the trade meeting. Imagine what the keentens will say when we tell them! We'll be invited into the sisterhood for sure."

Kay left the stall. She grabbed Alia's shoulders, rare delight on her face. "My apologies, Alia. My deepest apologies. Imorelle was right. She said you were cunning to try to get them to talk by giving them all they wished for, more cunning than she'd expected you to be. But I doubted you. I thought you were just being weak.

"They were at the trade meeting—that's worth giving them rags and a healer. You made a wise trade. I was the fool."

Alia shrugged, freeing her shoulders. It made her insides squirm to hear Imorelle's half-insulting praise, to imagine Kay talking of her so with Imorelle, to think of Imorelle going on and on over something she didn't understand at all. And for all Alia's effort, Kay still didn't see the meaning of what she had been trying to say. "Kay, you're not—" Alia started.

"Maybe after hearing your news, our Divin will finally decide to give the Beechians a strong punishment," Kay interrupted.

Surprised, Alia didn't say what she'd intended. "You don't think he'll be more likely to question them first?"

Kay shrugged, "Maybe, but it looks grimmer for them. First they were at the Blessed Groves. Then we found them skulking in Raven Wood. They're certainly not innocent travelers."

"But that's why we should question them. Why would spies be at a trade meeting?" Alia countered. "And they wouldn't have killed their own healers."

"Who knows what they'd do? Maybe now they don't want their healers, either. And truly, who cares?" Kay said with irritation.

"I care," Alia shot back. "I want to know the truth—don't you?"

"They're spies. *That's* the truth," Kay said, as if Alia had gone slow-witted. She started out of the Stables, saying over her shoulder, "Come on. Let's go tell the keentens what you've learned."

"Fine," Alia said. She pulled her cloak around her shoulders, her hands shaking with frustration. She had done all she could. If Kay looked foolish before the keentens, so be it.

They walked back out into the cold. Alia was glad Kay didn't speak with her or walk near her. She couldn't stand to hear one more of Kay's taunts or insults or pig-headed arguments.

But as they neared the Keenten House, foreboding settled heavily on Alia's shoulders. If Kay told the keentens how she had treated the Beechians, what would the warrior women do?

How would they punish her? Alia shook her head. Why did she care? Kay had made her own bed.

At the Keenten House, Jen greeted them with a smile. Without looking at each other, the girls followed her to the empty common room. When she turned to face them, Alia began her news of the Beechians.

Jen interrupted her, saying, "I'll fetch the Rinas." She put her hand on Alia's shoulder and added, "I knew you'd do well."

Alia welcomed the warmth from Jen's hand, and the warmth of the praise. The keentens' favor, at least, was something she need worry about no longer.

Kay crossed to the window and looked out, as if avoiding Alia. Alia went to the other side of the room, watching the doorway for the warrior women's entrance. They seemed to take their time. Alia wished they'd hurry. She glanced sideways at Kay. She wanted this done.

Soon two blue-scarfed Rinas came in the door. Kay turned from the window to listen as Alia explained what she had learned of the Beechians. From the upward turn of the Rinas' lips, Alia could tell they were pleased. Her spine straightened with pride.

The Rina who had judged the girls when the Beechians had first arrived, Rina Eleri, said, "This is what we have needed to push the Divin toward an execution."

Alia blinked. She thought she hadn't heard right. She asked, "Push the Divin toward an execution?"

The other Rina, a wiry woman named Fanelle, nodded. "He can't hesitate any longer. He'll hear from the master any day, and then we'll have our hangings," she said with satisfaction. "He was too cautious to begin with. We kept telling him he should have killed them long before this."

Alia stared at Rina Fanelle in horrified disbelief.

Ten

The Rinas wanted an execution.

Alia didn't move. The room felt hot and airless. The walls pressed in on her.

Alia's glance slid to Kay. For a moment Kay looked as astonished as she felt, but then her astonishment disappeared, as if the keentens' eagerness didn't matter at all. Kay nodded, agreeing with the Rinas. Alia looked back to the warrior women, feeling as if she were trapped inside a nightmare.

"It will be a glorious day for Loack to have made such a capture and brought down judgment so strongly," said Rina Fanelle. She smiled at Rina Eleri and added, "We usually don't show these to girls who aren't yet sisters, but come see the maps. They have all the places we fight—all the hills, streams, and forests between Loack and Beech." She gestured to the hides pinned to the walls.

Alia heard the words, the words that meant she would be a sister, but they seemed to get lost inside her. She couldn't feel anything, except that the room was too small and growing smaller all the time. "I need to get back," she finally managed to say. She ignored Kay, who shot a frown her way.

Rina Eleri laughed. "I hope you're as diligent with your chores when you enter this house." She bowed in dismissal. Alia turned quickly on her heel.

Once outside, Alia strode down the path without looking back. Kay caught up to her and pulled on her arm to stop her. "Didn't you hear them? We've proved our worth. We'll enter the sisterhood together."

"I heard them," answered Alia. "I heard everything they said."

Kay squeezed Alia's arm so hard that Alia had trouble hiding a wince. "What's wrong with you? Ever since the Beechians came, you've been acting strange. Imorelle said—"

"Who cares what Imorelle said? Imorelle doesn't know half as much as she thinks she knows," Alia said, wrenching her arm away.

"Imorelle knows a lot. A lot more than you do." Kay's voice was low and harsh. "She would never have said such things as you said. You were rude to the Rinas, *the Rinas*, Alia. They were going to do us an honor, and you refused it!"

"Did Imorelle know the keentens wanted an execution? Did *you* know they wanted one? That they were pushing the Divin toward one?" Alia asked, her own voice too high. She hated the sound of it.

"The keentens know better than us," Kay said, as if Alia had stepped too far. Her hands were tight, round fists and she looked as if she wanted to throw one of them at Alia, to force Alia to see things her way.

Alia felt a hollowness open up inside her, a deep, dark hollowness that had no bottom. Nothing she could say would make Kay understand her. Kay could do nothing to make Alia admit she was right. They were more like strangers than sisters.

And as if they were strangers, Kay bent her knees like a cat ready to pounce. Her cheeks flushed with anger and fight hunger. Alia's own legs tensed. The hollowness yawned wider. If Kay wanted a fight, she would have one.

A call interrupted them. It jolted Alia and she stepped away from Kay, ashamed of what they had almost done. Kay stepped away as well, as if also clutched by shame.

Both girls turned and saw Papa waving his arm and calling from the Smithy's back door. "I'll see you," said Kay, with a savage sullenness. She began to walk away.

"I'll see you," Alia answered. Though they hadn't touched each other, she felt bruised and stupid and furious. She wished that Papa weren't near. She didn't want him to ask what was wrong. She didn't want to have to explain.

She went to him, refusing to look over and see where Kay had gone. Papa said to her, "Had some business here. Thought I'd meet you and take you home after, though I expected you'd be coming from the Stables. I almost didn't see you."

"We had to tell the keentens something," answered Alia. She glanced at the Smith's door. She couldn't go in and listen to the men joke with the Smith; they would all expect her to smile and laugh. Some barrels and scraps of wood were piled against the stone building. "I'll sit out here until you're ready to leave," she said, pointing to them.

Papa studied her a moment, smoothing his beard with one hand. He shrugged. "If you want." Then he went back inside.

Alia rested against a barrel and stared out at the fields and firewood forests beyond the Keenten and Warrior Houses. Her breath came in big gulps. She put her hands over her face, forcing tears not to fall. She wouldn't cry. She wouldn't cry. Even if she and Kay never talked again, she wouldn't ever cry.

She dropped her hands and glared at the

snowy Keenten House, her house. She would fight and run free outside. She would win glory. But she would also have to do as the Rinas said, even if she thought them wrong. And Imorelle would be bragging over every one of her triumphs, all the while whispering with Kay. Alia imagined Kay leaning her head close to Imorelle's, listening, smiling, turning so she could whisper her own jokes and secrets in Imorelle's ear. The image, so clear and bright and painful, made Alia want to scream. She grabbed up a scrap of wood in the pile that lay next to the barrels. She hurled it as far as she could toward an empty field. And another piece. And another. Nothing was what she had thought it would be.

Alia stopped throwing only when the pieces of wood left beside her were large and awkward. She shook her hair back from her sweating face. She and Kay would have to find a way to stand together without fighting. Just as she would have to find a way to obey the Rinas. Somehow. She wiped her running nose with the back of her hand. But how?

High above her, rooks called to each other from the treetops, interrupting her thoughts. Their throaty calls made her belly squeeze—the grand mams said rooks gossiped together of who would soon die. Alia stared grimly at the soot-black birds flying circles in the overcast sky. Even the rooks knew there would be an execution.

Rhys and Kyrra didn't yet know. Kay wouldn't tell them. The keentens wouldn't, either. She'd do it now and run home. Maybe if she ran hard, until her breath came fast, the bleak ache in her chest would have no room to grow.

Alia went to the Smithy door, wanting to get her errand over and done. The Smith was showing Papa, Farmer Speare, and the Trader something by the light of the glowing fires. They didn't notice her leaning in the doorway.

"Papa," Alia called. All the men looked to her as she said, "I need to return to the prison for something. I'll meet you at home."

Papa came toward her, his hands tucked into his armpits. "All right," he said, though it seemed as if he was waiting for her to tell him more.

Alia looked beyond him to the other men. They had turned back to the Smith, but Alia didn't doubt that each had an ear cocked her way. She didn't feel like sharing her troubles with the whole village.

"I'll be home soon," she said, as if nothing were wrong.

Papa said, "Your mam'll be waiting on you."

Alia told him she'd hurry, then left. She would have time enough to explain herself to him later, away from all the wagging tongues.

Alia ran over the paths. When she reached the Prisoner House, she gave Kerrin the briefest of greetings. She walked to the cell and stopped without entering. She hated the words she had to say.

"The keentens will be coming for you," Alia said in a flat voice.

Rhys jumped up. He asked, "When? Now?"

"I'm not sure. We told the keentens you were at the Blessed Groves. Now they're sure you're spies. They want this to end soon," Alia said.

Kyrra nodded, but Rhys wanted more. "End how? With a questioning? With an execution?" he asked.

"Probably an execution," Alia said. The word "execution" tasted bitter on her tongue. "I just came to tell you."

"We need to speak," said Rhys.

"Rhys," Kyrra said, as if to a child who was walking too close to danger.

"It's the reason we came," said Rhys.

"What is?" asked Alia. He was near her now, his hands holding the bars as if he were trying to pull them open.

"Rhys, enough," Kyrra said. "You're going too far."

Alia stared at Rhys, caught by the hope and desperation in his golden-yellow eyes. He said to her, "We found a button at the grove where the healers burned. It belonged to none of the healers, and it was in the circle of flames, beyond where the other healers or the warriors could have stood to fight the fire. It could only belong to one of the killers.

"We've been searching and searching for anyone who might recognize the button, passing messages through the Healer Route. We finally received an answer from here, Loack. That's why we came."

"What Healer Route? What kind of an answer?" Alia asked. Rhys's words made no sense. She broke away from his stare and looked at Kyrra, whose face was filled with rage.

"Rhys, you never think. This is why you're here to begin with," Kyrra said in a low voice. "Not everyone knows about the Route. Look at her. She doesn't trust us. You may have just ruined everything."

"Show her the button, Kyrra. She's decent, you know she is. Maybe she can help us," said Rhys.

Alia waited for Kyrra to speak, holding back the questions tumbling through her. Kyrra stared at her brother and Alia. Then, slowly, she loosened the pouch at her neck. She reached in with two fingers and pulled something out. She held up the object for Alia to see.

Alia inhaled as if she had been struck in the

stomach. In the flickering lantern light, the patterns on the silver button seemed to swirl and writhe. It was a distinctive button, easily recognizable because the Smith had made it only on request. For the Divin.

"You found that at the burned grove?" Alia asked, her voice rough.

"When we went back, it was in the ashes," said Kyrra.

"Your healer friend saw it already. She told us it belongs to your divin," Rhys added.

"My healer friend?" Alia asked. The button was glinting in the light. She couldn't look away from it.

"Mari," said Rhys.

"Mari," Alia repeated. She was trying to think of a way the Divin's button could have reached the Blessed Groves, a way Beechians could have found it. She could think of no way. The Divin claimed, with pride, never to have been to Beech, not even before the war. And she had never seen buttons like it anywhere else. Not on a warrior. Not on a divin's apprentice. Not on anyone but Divin Ospar.

Alia couldn't move. The Divin had helped to burn the healers with magic. He had broken the Sacred Laws. He had broken his oaths. Alia felt her world was peeling away, leaving something underneath that she did not recognize.

Down the hallway, the door banged open, startling her. She heard booted feet in the hallway. She turned and saw, as if he had been summoned by their conversation, the Divin.

He strode toward Alia, looking as he always had: grand, majestic, and wise. The Beechians were wrong. They had to be.

Eleven

It was the Divin's jaw that made Alia hesitate. One muscle twitched and jumped as it had the day Mari angered him. Alia's gaze slid down to his tunic buttons. They were silver with spiraling designs, almost identical to the button Kyrra had hidden in her pouch. Anguish and uncertainty spilled through her. Why had Divin Ospar killed those healers?

"Why are you here at this time of day?" he asked with clear displeasure.

"I came back because I thought I left something here," Alia answered. She was surprised at how calm she sounded. Every word felt strange in her mouth.

"They didn't take anything from you, did they?" The Divin fixed his gaze on Rhys and Kyrra.

"No," Alia said, watching his eyes glitter as he looked at the Beechians. "I have a hole in my tunic pocket. Mam's luck stone fell from it."

Alia reached under her cloak, as if searching for the imaginary stone. Through her tunic, she could feel the outline of Raven Wood's leaf. Both her hand and her chest suddenly felt a painful coldness, as if the leaf were leaking icy breath. A shiver cut up the back of Alia's legs. The leaf didn't trust the Divin either.

"Ah, a luck stone," said the Divin. He never once looked away from Rhys and Kyrra. It was as if he couldn't. "I was pleased to hear your news about the Beechians. We've discovered little about those who burned the grove, and so I came directly over to speak with the prisoners. They might have caught a glimpse of the killers."

Alia stood straighter, as if readying herself for a fight. "So you'll call a questioning soon? My mam and papa are eager to hear what the prisoners will say," she said.

The muscle in the Divin's jaw twitched without pause. "I'll call a meeting to announce their punishment after I hear from the masters. This day, I'm going to question them here, alone."

The leaf's chill seared Alia's chest. "But shouldn't we all hear what they have to say?" she asked, each word clear and strong.

The Divin's stare turned on Alia. She met it without flinching. "I'll think on that," he said quietly. He ran one hand across his high forehead. "I see no luck stone here. Why don't you start home? I need to continue my work."

Alia kept her face still, though panic made her thoughts race. What would the Divin do to the Beechians once he had them alone? "I will after I stop at the Herb House," Alia said, looking over to Rhys. He had to understand what she was trying to do. "Their slop bucket was disgusting this morn. I think the boy is ill. I hope it isn't gut rot."

Rhys slumped, his arms pressed around his stomach. Alia held her breath, hoping the Divin wouldn't doubt him.

"Ah," said the Divin again. He smiled at Alia with his teeth, but not his eyes.

Alia turned her back on the Divin, half expecting him to stop her. As she walked away, the icy cold from her chest sank into her bones. Rhys and Kyrra were in danger each moment they were alone with the Divin—she had no time for long explanations to the keenten guard.

Alia stopped before the guard's chair, wishing she needn't lie. "The Divin is questioning the Beechians, but the boy has gut rot. I'm going for a healer. I'm hoping the boy won't heave his morn meal before we return."

Kerrin looked up at the ceiling and said, "Of course I have duty when they have some disgusting illness." She paused, then added, "I suppose

I'll have to go back and tend to the boy so the Divin needn't. Be quick, will you?"

"Of course," Alia answered, her hand already pulling at the door.

Alia let the door slam shut behind her and ran to the village center. She dodged and swerved past farmwives and artisans' apprentices, who all seemed to walk slower than mud turtles. Then she raced over the bridge, ignoring an irritated yelling coming from behind her. At the Herb House, she knocked loud and long until the gray-haired healer Narisse let her in.

Mari was at the Sick Room fireplace, stirring something in a pot. Alia stopped next to her. Other people were in the room: healers; Farmwife Bold and her sick children. Who knew about the Divin and who didn't? Standing with her back to the others so she couldn't be overheard, Alia said softly, "The Divin is alone with the prisoners, and I need to speak with you about a button."

Without stopping her work, Mari glanced up at Alia. Alia stepped back. Mari's skin was sallow. Her forehead held worry's creases. It was as if she had aged many cycles of the seasons in only a few days.

Mari looked down again as if Alia had told her about nothing more important than the thickness of the river's ice. She called out to the healer across the room, "Illana, someone needs to visit the prison again."

Illana, a plump woman in her middle years, walked to Mari and bent over, as if to examine the syrup in the pot. Mari whispered, "The Divin is alone with the Beechians."

"I told him they may have gut rot," Alia added. She studied the two women. Their concern was well hidden from the ailing in the room, showing itself only in small signs: Mari pulling at a curl of hair, Illana clasping and unclasping her hands. How long had they kept this secret? What other secrets did they have?

"I'll take the most noxious-smelling potions to the prison. That should drive him off," said the older woman, with a grim smile.

As Illana hurried away, Mari said to Alia, "We can't talk here. Give me a moment."

Alia couldn't stand to watch Mari stir syrup as if nothing this day were any different from any day that had come before. "I'll wait outside." She left with long, quick strides.

Once outside, Alia paced. She walked the length of the Herb House and the herbarium, then turned to look at the door. It hadn't moved. "Come on, Mari," she mutered. "Hurry yourself, for once."

She turned back and rounded the corner of the herbarium, then started toward the shack, the Speaker's Shack. She circled it, though it was bigger than she had thought, like a small house. As she rounded its last corner, she heard the Herb House door slam. "Finally."

But it had been someone going in, not Mari coming out. Alia strode the length of the herbarium again, then the length of the Herb House, and stopped under the oak tree by the door. The great tree's boughs were empty of leaves: it was no kin to Raven Wood. Still, it was like a vigilant warrior, watching over the Herb House. It seemed to frown down on Alia's restless irritability. She hunkered down to wait.

Movement on the bridge caught her attention. She looked down and saw two girls crossing. The taller girl leaned and stomped and the smaller, slighter girl did the same. Alia froze. It was Kay and Imorelle. They were trying to see who could knock the other onto the guide ropes, just as she and Kay always did. Or had done. Not lately. Not for a long while now.

Alia heard Kay's laughter ringing out over the snow. The laughter cut into Alia, sharp and twisting. Her teeth clenched so tightly they ached. How little Kay cared about their fight.

The Herb House door banged open. "Alia," said Mari, pulling a cloak over her shoulders.

"What?" Alia looked up, confused.

Then she remembered why she was sitting out here waiting for Mari. She stood and slapped snow from her leggings, her palms stinging from the force of her slaps. If Kay didn't care, she wouldn't care. And Kay could learn of the Divin from the keentens. "I'm ready," Alia told Mari, without looking toward the bridge. "Where are we going?"

"Sophia Wood," answered Mari. "I sent someone with a message to your mam and papa explaining that I needed you and that you'd be home late."

Sophia Wood was where the healers held ceremonies and collected herbs. The Divin, like all the other villagers, went to the wood for ceremonies but for nothing else. No one, not even the Divin, would overhear them there. "Let's go," said Alia.

Mari hurried away from the village, past the healers' well and wood stack and sleeping gardens. Her snow walkers seemed to skim over the snow. Alia was glad for Mari's speed, but was also surprised by it. She didn't remember Mari ever being so quick. There seemed to be much she didn't know about her cousin.

Sophia Wood was soon before them. Its leaves were a bright scarlet, with silver edges, stems, and veins. Each tree's trunk was so thick, a man couldn't reach his arms around it. Alia longed to put out a hand and run her fingers over the ridged bark, longed to stand and study the scarlet-and-silver leaves. The leaf in her pocket seemed to recognize the wood; it felt as if a sparkling liquid ran through it, making Alia's chest itch dreadfully. Mari didn't stop, though, so Alia scratched and ran to catch up to her cousin.

They traveled deep into the wood's shadows, but Mari showed no signs of slowing. Alia glanced at the majestic trees standing silently around her. The Beechians' secret was important, but she and Mari were now far from anyone who might overhear them.

"Mari," said Alia.

Mari didn't even turn to acknowledge her.

"Mari," Alia repeated with annoyance. "Don't you think we're safe enough here?"

Mari ran toward a pile of boulders that vied with the trees for height. She slowed as she approached a slab of rock. After speaking a few unintelligible words, she pulled the rock slab away from the other boulders. "Go in," she said, gesturing to the opening.

Alia bent over and peered into the cave. It was dark as the night's belly. "Is this a joke?" she asked. "I'm not going another step. You can explain here about the Beechians."

Mari rubbed one hand across her forehead. "Please go in. It's the only place we can talk safely. He could find us anywhere but in the tunnels."

Alia looked at Mari. Worry lines crowded

around the healer's mouth. Her large black eyes were wary and watchful. Alia's anger seeped away. Mari knew more of this than she did. Without another word, Alia removed her snow walkers and ducked into the cave.

The path descended into the earth, becoming a tunnel. Alia crouched so her head wouldn't bump the ceiling. Behind her, she could hear Mari coming in and closing the entrance. Then lantern light broke through the darkness.

Alia absently scratched at her itching chest and looked around, fascinated. Tree roots wove through the earthen ceiling and walls, as if Sophia Wood had shaped the tunnel itself. Every few steps, stone arches rose up and crossed the ceiling. Alia saw faint outlines of carvings on the arches' stones, as well as in alcoves that held unlit lanterns.

Soon the passageway was tall enough that she could stand straight. It opened into a large round room with several new paths branching from it. Alia stopped, uncertain where Mari would want to go.

The healer slipped ahead and hung the lantern on a hook. Then she turned to face Alia. "What's wrong with your chest? Why do you itch at it so?" she asked.

Alia laughed in disbelief. "We have more important things to talk of, Mari," she said.

"I'll be distracted if you're always scratching," said Mari. "And I could help you."

"This is silly," said Alia as she reached into her tunic pocket for the leaf. "It's only . . . " Her voice trailed away.

The pocket was empty. Alia's hand hesitated. Through the wool, she could feel the leaf's outline. Curious and a little fearful, she reached inside her undertunic. She found no leaf. On her skin were the ridges of the leaf's edges and veins, but the leaf itself was gone. It seemed to have melted into her.

"Mari," Alia said, her voice sounding too loud.

Mari came to Alia and helped her pull down her undertunic's collar enough so they could see better. Above Alia's heart was the leaf's outline. Delicate golden veins rose over her skin, and the skin between the veins was slightly orange. The golden stem curved down, pointing toward her rib cage.

"What happened to me? This used to be a leaf. It dropped from Raven Wood and I put it in my pocket," said Alia in awe. She traced the ridges, and they tingled under her touch.

Mari shook her head and peered at the mark. "I've seen nothing like this before. There's a story of Roanna, a healer in the Old Tales. She had 'leaves emblazoned on both palms.' I assumed that meant skin paints." Mari leaned closer. "Perhaps not."

Alia stared at the mark, running her fingers over it. Her skin, and yet different. Thrilled and spooked, she couldn't tear her gaze from it.

"You should show the Eldress," Mari said.

"The Eldress." Alia's hand covered the mark. She didn't want the Eldress poking and prodding at her. "Would she know what it is?"

"I'm sure she would. Though it is an odd thing."

Alia gave a brusque nod. She doubted Mari was right. Even the Divin knew little of Raven Wood.

The Divin.

Alia let her undertunic and tunic slide back up to her neck. Her hands tightened into fists. "Mari, we can talk more of the mark later. I want to know about the button."

Mari nodded, staring at the lantern's flickering light. The worry lines on her forehead and around her mouth grew deeper. "The button. Well. Soon after the trade meeting, the Beechians sent a message through the Healer Route that said they had found a button in the grove's ashes. I recognized the description and asked if we could see it," said Mari. She smiled sadly. "Divin Ospar has such distinctive buttons.

"Kyrra is apprenticing to be a messenger, someone who carries messages around and out of Beech. Since her sister was one of those killed at the trade meeting, Kyrra insisted on bringing the button here. It was her right to take the task, though since she's only apprenticed, she need not have come. She knew she might be captured and killed; I suspect she was sure she would be. But Kyrra would leave the task to no one else, for she thought no one cared as much as she that someone here know the truth and try to do something about it." Mari continued, her voice very tired. "She thinks so poorly of the masters and Magus that she didn't even consider going to them. She really believes they wouldn't be troubled, as we would, that our divin did such a thing."

Alia tried to take all this in, every incredible word of it. "And Rhys?"

"Rhys was not supposed to come. He followed Kyrra and revealed himself only once she was too far along to turn back. He wouldn't turn back, either. He wanted, I think, to protect her." Mari smiled a bit. "He's an impulsive boy."

Alia leaned against one of the stone arches. Its unyielding coolness steadied her. "But what do you mean you 'sent a message'? What's the Healer Route?" she asked.

Mari tucked her hands into the sleeves of her robe. "It's in the Sacred Laws: healers speak regardless of war, feast, or famine. We meet and speak of potions and spells and herbs. It's important to our work. But there have been times, such as now, when the Magus and his Divinhood haven't wanted us to speak as much as we do. They forbid it, so we use the secret paths and tunnels, like this one and the one near which you found Rhys and Kyrra. The divins assume we speak with Beechians rarely—only to arrange trade meetings."

Alia thought of Rhys's music, of Kyrra's bravery, of her slain elder brothers, of the Divin's evil. A hard knot seemed to lodge just below her rib cage. Rhys and Kyrra had come all this way, had walked into danger, to face her own divin. Her divin. Who had hidden his face and killed with magic. "Why did Divin Ospar do this?" Alia asked, fiercely.

"I don't know. Maybe something has twisted in him. I've seen warriors like that—so eaten up by hate that they don't know right from wrong. I can't tell," said Mari again. She turned to Alia, her shoulders slumping. "And since I found out about the Divin, I've wondered about the horrible things the Beechian healers have told us of the divins in their villages. We always assumed their stories were lies." Her voice was very low as she said, "Maybe they were speaking some truth."

Alia's skin prickled with gooseflesh. She stood up straight. "It isn't like that. It can't be. My brothers had missions in Beech. They would never have fought on if they had found that divins there betrayed the Sacred Laws. Never."

Mari stared at the shadowy ground. Her thoughts seemed suddenly very far away. "After we were promised to each other, my Ewan often had to go to Beech. If he had seen that the divins had grown evil, he wouldn't have fought on and died there, either. Though I didn't hear much from him in the end." Mari's words faded into silence. She stood very still, as if lost in her memories. Then she said, "But Beech is not our concern right now. *Our* divin has broken his oaths. He's killed healers and one of the Blessed Groves."

Alia thought of how Divin Ospar had pretended to condemn the burning. He had made the trap. He had called up the fire. He watched the leaves curl and burn and heard the cries for help and had—what? Rejoiced? Alia fought down the urge to retch.

"So what have you and the other healers done about all this?" she asked.

"We sent a message to the masters, but we've received no reply yet. While we've waited, we've wanted to show the keentens the button. We don't often challenge the Divin openly. When he forbids certain spells to healers because we're women, we use the spells secretly in times of dire need. When he forbids us to speak with healers in Beech, we're careful to hide our travels. But this is different. We need to stand and speak against him, and we need others to stand with us. Few would listen to a healer speak against a divin."

"But you haven't yet shown the keentens the button?" Alia asked, perplexed.

Mari shook her head. "Kyrra won't speak with the keentens. She thinks they would rather kill her than shame their divin."

"The keentens want the Beechians dead," Alia said, unable to keep some bitterness from her voice, "but they wouldn't do that. If they saw the button, they would demand the Divin answer for it."

"I agree with you, but Kyrra doesn't trust them," Mari said. "I just keep hoping that the masters will advise a questioning, maybe even come here to witness it. Then they would see that they must take the Divin to the Magus for a trial. And they wouldn't execute Rhys and Kyrra as spies."

"Mari, the Divin knows Rhys and Kyrra were at the groves now. He'll try to make sure the masters never see them. You have to tell the keentens as soon as you can, no matter what Kyrra wants."

Mari nodded, but her look was bleak. "If I can."

"You will. I'll help you," Alia said. "Kyrra has to see that speaking with the keentens is her last hope."

"I've been so worried over this I'm not able to think straight," said Mari with a flicker of a smile. "If you think you can convince Kyrra, I'd be glad of your help."

From far back in the tunnel, they heard the scrape of the stone doorway. Mari and Alia both froze where they stood.

"Mari," a voice called into the tunnel. "Come up. The Eldress wishes us all back in the Herb House. The Divin has called a meeting about the prisoners for this eve."

"This eve," echoed Mari. Then she called, "We're coming."

Alia and Mari walked quickly through the tunnel. At the cave's mouth, they met Ana, a healer with long silver-streaked hair. Ana frowned at Alia but said nothing. Then she turned to lead them from the wood.

Alia and Mari put on their snow walkers, then filed through the trees without speaking. Ana kept looking behind her, as if she thought they might not be alone. After several strange noises, Ana stopped, wordlessly pulling Mari and Alia behind a tree. Alia looked into the wood, searching. The mark on her chest, her leafprint, was silent—no chill, no tingling, nothing. Still, unease settled between her shoulder blades.

The third time they stopped, Alia knew they were being followed. Twigs behind them continued cracking, as if broken by someone taking a few more steps. Cold, unbearable cold, suddenly filled Alia's leafprint. She could see no one in the wood's shadows, but her mouth went dry.

"It must be the Divin," Mari whispered. "Who else would follow us?"

"Why doesn't he strike us with magic?" breathed Alia. Her heart fluttered so in her chest, she thought it might lift her from the ground.

The answer returned to her in the same soft whispering. "Magic is unpredictable in woods and groves. It takes incredible strength to ignore the trees' powers. At the Blessed Groves, he wasn't alone."

Alia nodded, then saw her suspicions reflected in the two other faces. Maybe the Divin wasn't alone here, either.

Alia, Mari, and Ana pressed on, twisting and turning so their route couldn't be predicted. Nothing they did hindered the one chasing them. His cracking steps grew closer. Without slowing her pace, Alia looked over her shoulder. Still she saw no one.

Alia and the healers neared the wood's edge. They ran faster, crashing and tripping over fallen trees and brush. He wouldn't dare touch them in the open. Someone might see him. They had to reach the field.

Suddenly, Alia struck something, and her face

and chest rang with pain. She reeled back, her arms wrapped around her aching body. Mari and Ana both fell against her. They all swayed; then Alia caught her balance. She helped the others steady themselves.

Alia reached one hand forward into what should have been empty space. The air between the trees was as solid as a wall.

"What is this?" she hissed.

"An air spell," Mari whispered back. "We're at the wood's edge and he's taking a chance."

Behind them, the cracking didn't stop. He was no longer stalking. He was hunting.

Twelve

Alia pushed against the invisible wall, trying to break through it with her shoulder. It didn't move. The footsteps sounded closer, but when she glanced behind her, she saw no one. She faced the wall and shoved. The wall still didn't move. Breathing hard, she struck at it with her fists.

She heard Mari say, "We'll have to pierce it."

"There's no time for that spell," argued Ana.

Alia stopped pounding at the wall. Fear overran her thoughts, splashing into every part of her, but she didn't give in to it. She dropped her mittens and, with her fingertips, searched the rigid air for weak spots. The invisible wall had peaks and swirls, like cream whipped thick, but no softness that she could find.

Alia thrust one foot and its snow walker at the wall. Her leafprint was now icy cold. She pressed her hands to the mark on her chest, trying to warm its aching chill. At her touch, the leafprint began to tingle.

Her foot sank back to the ground. Words murmured around her. Strange, ancient words. Hopeful words.

"Alia, take my hand," said Ana.

Alia heard Ana through a haze. She reached under her clothes and laid one palm on the leafprint. Liquid warmth ran through the mark's stem, then flooded up through its veins.

"They can help us," Alia said. Her own voice sounded far away.

"Who?" asked Mari.

Still touching the leafprint, Alia put her other hand on the tree next to her. She felt bark: rough, ridged, split with age. She closed her eyes. Underneath the bark was a slow flowing movement—lifeblood. Alia matched its pulse with both her breath and her heart.

The words became clearer, deep and resonant, almost a song. The tree spoke of the magic now in the wood, the Divin's forbidden magic. But interwoven were other harmonies—of the wind's journeys, of the moon's faces, of the birds' councils. Alia could not tell if these things were part of the Divin's evil or separate, whether they had happened in the past or would happen in the future. She wanted to listen on and on until the song was sung out to its end, but time was pressing her.

"Ystraid," Alia said to the tree. It was a word she had never said before, but somehow she knew its meaning. *Help*.

The tree hesitated and grew silent.

Heat blazed through Alia. It rose from her feet, ran up her legs, and seared out her fingertips. It was followed by something sharp, ripping at her, tearing her in two. She heard a cracking sound; then the heat left her. She sank to her knees.

Alia forced her heavy eyelids open. Nothing looked changed, but she knew the air wall before her had snapped. She stared at where it had been.

A hand yanked her away from the tree and dragged her up. She didn't realize it was Mari until she heard the healer's voice. "Move, Alia. We have to get to the Herb House."

Alia couldn't think what the trouble was, but she had no strength to fight Mari. With Mari holding one of her arms and Ana holding the other, she stumbled forward.

They left the wood for the field. The cold wind scraped at Alia's nose and cheeks. Her snow walkers slipped on the snow's frozen rind or broke through. Each time she fell, it was harder to rise.

Alia and the healers pushed on. Alia's hands and legs trembled. She tripped and fell. The icy crust broke, and she sank. She thought of lying down. Of pressing her cheek to the ground. Of drifting away.

Mari said in her ear, "You can't sleep here."

Alia didn't move. She felt hands on her arms.

"You can't. The wood is holding the Divin for now, but it won't hold him forever. And I won't let him have you," said Mari.

The Divin. Alia lifted her heavy head. The Divin had been hunting them. When the wood finally freed him, he might hunt them still. Well, he wouldn't catch them. She struggled up. One foot followed the other. She tried to help the healers as they half-dragged her past the gardens, past the woodshed, up to the Herb House.

They burst in the door, Mari and Ana still supporting her. The five other healers were clustered around the eating table. They looked up, veils askew, mouths open in surprise. Mari and Ana started removing Alia's outdoor clothes. She leaned against the wall and let them, too weary to care for her pride.

The Eldress rose from the group of healers, pushing herself up with her cane. "You're back. Good," she said, tersely. Then she said, "Come," and guided them to the kitchen.

Just inside the kitchen door, Alia sank to the floor and leaned against a barrel. The Eldress handed her a thick earthenware cup full of tea.

Alia had to remind her hand to reach out and close around the handle. In a hushed voice, Ana began to describe the chase, but Alia could barely follow her words.

Alia looked down into the tea. Red and green swirls circled through the mud-brown brew. She sipped, squinting against the liquid's vile taste. It burned down her throat into her belly, chasing away her fatigue. She blinked, her thoughts suddenly clear.

She had spoken to the trees in a language she had never heard before, had never even known existed. And the trees had spoken back—in words. Slipping her hand into her undertunic, she traced the leafprint's ridges. She felt as if she couldn't catch enough breath. What was this mark Raven Wood had given her?

The Eldress's rasping voice broke in on Alia's thoughts. "He must have strong suspicions to chase you." The healers were talking of the Divin. The Divin, who had tried to harm her with magic and whom the trees had called evil. She laid her hand flat against her leafprint—though her fingers itched to retrace and retrace it—and tried to listen better to the Eldress.

"I should have spoken with the keentens about the button, despite the Beechian girl's fears," said the Eldress, her mouth puckering into a sour expression. "The Divin has something planned. We must be on our guard, both before the meeting this eve and during it. And if he comes here searching for you, stay in the kitchen. I'll keep him away."

"We'll all go to the meeting?" asked Ana.

"We'll all go," the Eldress answered, keeping her voice low, as if the Divin might be eavesdropping at the door. "This may be our only chance to trap him. I'd feel better if the masters had answered our message and come."

Mari voiced the question in Alia's head. "The Beechians are safe?"

"For now," said the Eldress, pushing up her bent spectacles. "The boy has the most peculiar case of gut rot we've ever seen. None of our potions can touch it. He just lies there and moans pitifully. A healer has to sit right with him in the cell."

Alia couldn't help smiling. The Eldress and Mari smiled, too.

"Eldress, there's something else," Ana said. She gestured at Alia. "This girl spoke with the trees. That's how we escaped. The wood listened to her, then broke the spell trapping us and reached to hinder the Divin. I've never heard anything like the word she spoke, not in any spells, or laws, or stories."

They all looked at Alia, silent, waiting. The Eldress's clear, sharp stare held certainty; she knew of the trees' songs. Alia didn't know whether her palms were sweating from excitement or from fear.

But the Eldress only said, "Well? What explanation do you have? Hurry up with it. We don't have much time."

Alia pushed herself up with as much grace as she could manage. She almost walked away; the Eldress could play her games with someone else. But magic had cut through Alia, touching every bit of her. Magic from trees that could talk. She couldn't leave without answers, if there were any.

"I heard the tree speak words, and I asked the wood for help," Alia said, standing as tall and steady as she was able. "I don't know how I knew the right word to say."

She pulled down her tunic and undertunic, exposing the leafprint. Having it laid bare made her feel unclad and too vulnerable. "I think this is what helped me," she said.

The Eldress squinted at it. "I see." Then she folded her wrinkled hands on the head of her cane, and said, "It's a sign."

"A sign from whom? For what?" asked Alia.

"It's from the trees," answered the Eldress. "You're a speaker." She said it as if pointing out the obvious: you're a girl, you're Geoffrey's daughter, you're a Trantian.

"But speakers are rare," said Ana, her voice disbelieving. "No one has lived in our Speaker's House since before my grand mam was a child. And there are hardly any in the Magus's provinces."

"There have been few since the Dark Days," Mari explained to Alia, "when they and the healers had to hide because the Divinhood forbade women to use magic."

Alia wasn't interested in such details. "But what is a speaker?" she asked.

The Eldress studied her. "You've seen twelve springs, which is when the talent for magic starts to wake in a child. You have an affinity with the trees, an ability to hear them and speak with them. This is the sign they've given you that they've recognized and accepted you. You don't need to speak with them ever again if you don't wish to. Like any talent, it will die if you let it."

Alia thought of the song she had heard so little of. "Why would I let it die?"

Ana said, "You care nothing for healing or tending herbs. Speakers talk with the trees so they can pass the trees' knowledge on to healers. I don't understand why the trees even chose to recognize you."

"They see something they like in her," answered the Eldress.

Alia let her tunic and undertunic cover her

mark. The warmth she'd received from the healing drink had abandoned her. "So . . . speakers work with healers?"

"I could read to you of speakers in the Sacred Texts, and I could teach you some as well." The Eldress tilted her head. "But it's not the learning of keentens."

Alia was silent. Not the learning of keentens. Her place in the Keenten House was assured. But the learning of the trees was not the learning of keentens.

The Eldress stared at Alia as if her skin were as clear as glass and everything she thought and felt could be seen through it. "There's no need for you to join the Herb House. Most speakers are healers, but not all. They spend much of their time in the woods or groves, not in the herbarium or Sick Room. I probably wouldn't have you in my Herb House, in any case. You wouldn't suit it."

"No, I wouldn't." Alia folded her arms tightly across her chest. A speaker. Not a keenten—a speaker. Kay and Imorelle would fight for peace; they would be sisters. She would not. The thought made her feel ill—cold and hot and shaky.

So she would be a keenten, not a speaker. She wouldn't hear the trees' song again. The trees would never again pour their magic through her.

Her talent would die. She realized she was shaking hard now. "I . . . I need to think." She couldn't make herself say *I will not be a speaker.*

The door banged in the other room. Voices rose, and then Illana, the healer who had been tending the Beechians, hurried into the kitchen. Her expression was one of pure fright. Alia asked, "What is it? What's happened?"

"Divin Ospar is in the prison again. He made me leave," said Illana. "The Beechians are alone with him. I didn't even see a keenten guard when I left."

Alia was the first out the door, leaving everything—hat, mittens, cloak, snow walkers—inside the Herb House. Mari followed her, matching her step for step.

Alia's hair flew out behind her like a great dark wing. Her feet skidded over the paths. She and Mari crossed the bridge and the Road. They ran past the Inn and raced toward the Prisoner House, ignoring all who tried to slow them or ask them what was wrong.

Kay was on the path to the prison, a pot under one arm. For the first time in days, Alia was glad to see her. Whatever Kay's faults, she was fast. "We need help," Alia told Kay. "Get the keentens."

"What do you mean?" Kay said, astonished.

Mari pushed past them as the eve bell rang.

The bell's chimes made Alia's heart pound hard and painful against her ribs. If the Divin wished to harm Rhys and Kyrra, he would have done it before now, before Alia and Kay were supposed to arrive with the dinner. What if they were too late?

"There's no time, Kay. The Rinas. Get the Rinas. As quick as you can."

"I don't understand," Kay said, looking warily after Mari. "What is this about?"

Alia grabbed Kay's arm. "If you don't fetch the Rinas, we may not have any prisoners."

Kay didn't hesitate any longer. With a nod, she ran toward the Keenten House.

Alia stepped into the small front room. No guard was in sight. The Divin must have sent her away. Alia ran down the hallway, imagining Rhys and Kyrra unmoving on the floor. She reached the cell and stopped. Through the gloom, she could see that they were not on the floor, but the scene before her was little better.

Mari stood next to the Divin, her face full of shock and horror. The Divin was holding one hand out toward the Beechians. Rhys and Kyrra were absolutely still, as if frozen solid.

"Are they dead?" Alia asked, her voice scraping her throat.

The Divin turned to look at her. He smiled. A familiar, friendly smile, not evil in the least. She wondered if he practiced those smiles before he brought them out for all to see.

"Of course not," the Divin said. "The boy threatened me, so I defended myself with an air spell. It will hold them still, but nothing will happen to them before the meeting this night."

Alia looked to Rhys and Kyrra. She could see now that something was in their eyes, an awareness, an anguish. They could see and hear what was happening, but they could do nothing. It was as if the Divin wanted them to watch this, wanted them to be frightened. Disgust made it hard for Alia to swallow.

The Eldress and other healers, followed by Rina Eleri, Jen, and a few other keentens, pushed into the cell. Kay elbowed through the crowd to Alia.

"What is this about?" asked Rina Eleri.

Alia said, "The Eldress knows the whole tale. She can tell you."

The Rina arched one eyebrow, then turned to face the Eldress. Kay's lips parted with surprise. Then she shut her mouth. Her eyes scanned the room, narrowing. They came back to rest on Alia. "What is this, Alia?" Kay demanded in a fierce whisper. "Why did you tell me the prisoners needed our aid?"

"They do need our aid. Look at them. They're both still weak. Could they have truly attacked anyone?" Alia asked, but even as she said the words, she knew Kay would not agree.

"You're calling the Divin a liar." Kay's tone was threatening.

"Just watch." Alia crossed her arms and squeezed tight. For a moment, outside, things had seemed as before with Kay. Now Kay wouldn't listen, and everything was all wrong again.

"The Eldress," the Divin said severely, "I'm sure, has quite a tale to tell, but probably not the tale we need to hear." He dropped his hand and strode over to the Eldress. As he walked by Alia, she sucked in air as if she had been slapped. Across his cheeks were ragged red cuts in the shape of branches. She had known he had chased her through the wood, that the trees had answered her call and stopped him, but the clear proof on his face still chilled her blood.

"Why don't you tell our Rina who asked the Beechians here?" he challenged the Eldress.

"Divin," the Eldress answered. "I think the most important question is yet to be asked. Why did the Beechians come?"

Rina Eleri said in a low voice, "You didn't answer his question, healer."

"I think she's frightened to have the attention turning to her and her house. I've caught several healers using spells and powers forbidden to them," said the Divin. "An eldress could lose her robe and veil for such disregard of the Magus's rulings."

The Divin leaned over the Eldress. He spoke with a soft, certain outrage. "And before the boy attacked me, I found from him that you called these enemies here, into our village. Why do you betray us?"

Alia heard Kay inhale sharply. Alia opened her mouth to break in on his twisting of the truth, but Mari spoke before her. "I sent for the Beechians," she said.

The Rina's lips grew thin. The muscles in her neck were stretched tight, as if all of her was ready to lash out in judgment. Mari continued, her words tumbling over themselves. "I sent for them because we had word that the Beechians had found something at the Blessed Groves."

"You knew of this?" Kay whispered at Alia. "What is she babbling about? The healers 'had word' from whom? If the Beechians found something in the groves, why did they never say anything of it before?"

"You wouldn't believe me if I told you," Alia answered with bitter certainty. "When you see for yourself what they have, you'll understand."

"I may understand if I see it, but not if you tell me of it. You make no sense," Kay snapped. She turned her shoulder to Alia as if it were a wall, turned toward the Divin.

Alia stepped up next to Kay so they were shoulder to shoulder. She wanted to see Kay's face when Kyrra showed the button. She wanted to see Kay realize that she had tried to tell her the truth, as she had tried so often in the past days.

"They told me nothing of a finding at the groves," said the Divin to Mari, his jaw twitching.

"Loose Kyrra, and she'll show you," said Mari.

"You know their names, healer?" asked Jen, as if this in itself proved Mari was a traitor.

Mari said again, "Loose Kyrra. It will explain everything."

Rina Eleri's voice was sharp. "I'm sure the Divin, like me, wants to see what the prisoners have to show us. The Divinhood has found little during its pursuit of the grove killers. Though why the Beechians bring their find here, I don't understand."

She turned to the Eldress, her tone growing harsher. "Then I, and I'm sure all of us, want to hear how the Beechians came here."

The Divin looked down at the Eldress. He interlaced his fingers over the shimmering silver embroidery on his tunic. The rest of his clothes—his cape, his trousers, his boots—all blended with the darkness in the room, as if he were half made of shadow.

"Yes, we all want to know more of what happened at the Blessed Groves," said the Divin.

"But I fear the Beechians' 'find' will be nothing but a ploy to deceive us. They deceived the Eldress with it already. Or used it to buy her allegiance."

The Divin held up one hand. Alia heard a rushing sound and watched Rhys and Kyrra closely, prepared for a trick from the Divin. The Beechians swayed, then reached for the wall to hold themselves up. They looked weak, but awake. Alia's spirits soared. Perhaps the Divin did not realize the danger he was in.

The Divin warned, "The boy tried to attack me. I would be prepared for a trick."

The keentens circled the Beechians, and Kay stepped forward as well. Alia stared past the hard bodies, the stony expressions, the polished daggers. Rhys brushed back his hair, his hands awkward without their flute. Kyrra gripped her neck pouch with one hand. Alia waited eagerly for them to speak.

"Kyrra," said Mari. "Show what's in the pouch."

Kyrra looked at Mari as if she didn't understand. Mari waited. The Beechian girl said nothing.

"The pouch, Kyrra," Mari said.

Kyrra gazed around the room, her attention drifting from one person to the next. She looked like a drowsy, overgrown child.

Mari turned to the Divin. Her voice was low and slightly unsteady as she said, "What have you done to them?"

"It's a regrettable effect of the spell. It'll wear off eventually," said the Divin with a smile. "It takes a bit for them to thaw out." Laughter rippled among the keentens. Kay's laughter was as loud as the rest.

A whirlpool of anger spun through Alia. Her brothers had fought and died for justice, not so their divin could break laws and oaths and kill.

The whirlpool sucked Alia forward and the laughter ended abruptly. She ignored Kay's amazement and the keentens' narrow-eyed, tight-lipped scowls. She ignored Rhys, his hands hanging clumsy by his sides as if they would never play music again. She ignored the empty, lost look Kyrra wore.

Alia took Kyrra's elbow and led her forward through the ring of warriors. She had to slow to match Kyrra's tentative steps. They stopped near Divin Ospar. He watched them with an impatient frown.

The Divin's impatience only angered Alia more. She loosened Kyrra's hand from the pouch. Reaching into the small leather bag, she sorted through its strange scraps: pebbles, bits of bark, and other things she didn't recognize by touch. Then she found the button.

Alia looked over at Kay. Kay's amazement had gone. Her arms were crossed and her mouth was pressed shut. She stood as all the keentens stood, angry and watchful. Alia pinched the button so her fingers hurt. A tree had listened to her, but Kay and the keentens, her sisters, wouldn't. Well, they would have to. She pulled her hand from the pouch and held the button high. "This is what they found in the ashes of the grove that burned," Alia said.

Kay stared. All the keentens stared. Eyes glittering. Mouths dark and open. It was as if they expected the button to snarl at them. Then Rina Eleri said, haltingly, "That . . . I believe that button is yours, Divin." She paused, and to Alia's horror, gave a light laugh as if this were all a misunderstanding. "But how could they have it?"

For an endless moment, Alia stood frozen. The button was the Divin's. He claimed never to have been to Beech. These Beechians had it. Yet the Rina would look away from the truth, waiting for any excuse the Divin gave. The other keentens, and Kay, too, waited as well, silent. Alia felt as if something sharp had been thrust into her stomach.

The Divin turned to Alia, a slight smile drawing up the corners of his mouth. A raw, bleak chill spread through her as he spoke. "The Beechians couldn't have found that at the groves. I wore it only this morn."

Thirteen

"I lost the button earlier this day but never thought to look in the cell. I don't know why Alia chooses to believe what the enemies told her," said the Divin. His smile disappeared. "She's either dull-witted or a traitor."

"I'm neither," Alia said from within her bleak chill.

The Rina and the keentens looked on her with grave disapproval, unconvinced. Kay stood with the warrior women, staring at her as if at a stranger. Alia felt cold creep into the marrow of her bones.

"The Beechians described this button to me two moons ago," Mari said to the Divin. "You've never gone to Beech and these children have never been to Trant. How would they know of your buttons if they hadn't found one in the burned grove?"

"Did you devise this plan, healer?" the Divin

asked Mari. "When you asked the spies to come, was it already your thought to try to ruin me with your lies?"

"That's not what happened," Mari protested, her voice loud in the small crowded cell.

The keentens said nothing, studying Mari with looks as sharp as daggers. And Kay was just like them. Watching Alia. Not believing. Accepting the Divin's lies.

Horror dried Alia's mouth. She could see the healers felt it, too; Illana's arms were folded tightly across her chest, the Eldress's hands squeezed her cane's knobby head, Mari was shaking. Behind them stood Ana and the others, fear in their faces. But no healer dropped her head or backed away. They would not let this struggle end here. Despite her horror, Alia almost felt like laughing. What a fool she had been to think the healers weak. What a fool Kay was.

"The girl speaks the truth, Divin," said the Eldress. "You can't pretend you lost the button this morn. Just after the fire in the Blessed Groves, the Beechians sent word of it all around. We will not have been the only ones to recognize it as yours. You frequently visit other villages."

"Don't dig deeper into this mire, Eldress," the Divin said. "You can't save yourself, or the girl, with falsehoods."

The keentens murmured in agreement, already

condemning the Eldress. Alia's leafprint pulsed, chasing the outraged desperate beat of her heart. She said to the Divin, "You couldn't have lost that button this morn. When I saw you earlier, you were wearing just what you're wearing now."

The Divin shook his head. "You know I wasn't. What makes you lie?"

Before Alia could retort, another voice spoke. "Alia doesn't lie." Stunned, Alia realized the voice was Kay's.

"This isn't for you to decide," the Rina snapped.

Kay stood tall and stiff. She cast a sideways glance at Alia, then to the Divin, then her eyes went back to Alia. Angry, uncertain eyes. More angry and uncertain than Alia had ever seen them. They fixed on the Divin again. "Yes, Rina. But Alia doesn't lie."

Alia's mouth dropped open. She had never heard Kay contradict a keenten, let alone a Rina.

"We'll decide if she is or isn't a liar," the Rina said, her voice severe.

"Yes, Rina." Kay's blazing eyes went to Alia, though. She gave the slightest of nods, acknowledging Alia had been right.

Alia was frozen, unable to move. Kay had believed her. Believed so strongly that she had risked the Rina's displeasure to speak up.

Kay's eyes pulled at Alia. Through every trouble, they had always stood together. They still should stand together. Together as sisters. Together as keentens. Alia leaned forward, as if to take a step. But her feet didn't move.

Her hands squeezed into fists. Squeezed so hard her palms hurt. Or at least one palm. She opened her fingers; she was still holding the Divin's button. The flickering lantern light shone off it, making its pattern seem to spiral and writhe. Something about it tugged at Alia. She stared at the flat, circular bit of silver, mesmerized.

The keentens talked, the healers argued, Kay still stared, but Alia couldn't look away from the button.

The button. So strange. Its pattern, unique.

Unique.

A unique button. Made at the Divin's request. Made by the Smith.

"The Smith," she said. "Ask the Smith if the Divin requested he replace the button."

Every face jerked toward her, except for Rhys's and Kyrra's.

"I lost the button only this morn," the Divin answered scathingly. "I haven't requested he replace it." Under the raw scratches on one cheek, his jaw muscle twitched without stop.

That muscle made Alia know she had found

what she had sought. "If I'm wrong, what does it matter if we ask?" she said into the breathless silence.

Rina Eleri walked over and stood before Alia. Alia tilted her head and looked into the warrior woman's thin, beautiful face. The Rina's voice lashed out. "Why do you press this? If even a rumor creeps out that Divin Ospar was one of the killers, people will forget all his wisdom and speak only poison of him and our village. Would you stand with the enemy and have this happen?"

Alia looked at Kay, who stood silent, her eyes ablaze. Her heart clenched tight and she could barely breathe. Kay would stand with Rina Eleri. Kay would be a sister.

Alia looked back at the Rina. She could not. Not this day. Not ever.

"Yes, I would stand with the Beechians." The words tore from Alia, making her throat ache. "Our divin killed healers. He killed the Blessed Grove. Yet you would rather blame me than him. I thought you fought for truth."

The Rina's face became as smooth and hard as stone. Kay's face, too, was rigid. Rigid and angry and unrelenting. Alia felt as if she had fallen into a narrow stifling well. Alone.

"If you will not ask the Smith of the button, I will." Alia heard someone say. She realized it was herself. No one answered her, but a whistling sound filled the room. Alia looked toward it. What she saw stopped all her anguish and arguments. The Divin was raising his hands. Alia's leafprint instantly became biting cold. She was surrounded by rushing air. "No!" she cried.

The air around her grew strong. It squeezed her feet and legs. She thought she might crumple within its crushing grip.

"What are you doing?" yelled the Rina to the Divin.

"I'm protecting you," the Divin snapped.

Alia tried to reach out to the Rina, to the Eldress, to Kay or Mari or anyone. The air pinned her arms to her sides. It tangled her hair around her face.

"He's lying," cried Kay. "He's hurting Alia."

Then Alia couldn't hear. The air pressed into her ears and mouth and eyes. She choked and gasped. He was cutting her off from life.

Everything grew hazy and began to close into darkness.

Then the tightening air vanished so abruptly, Alia stumbled from its sudden absence. Someone caught her arm and steadied her. Alia sucked in deep, shaking breaths. The darkness receded. Light and sound and smell came back to her. Her leafprint warmed, sending heat to her chilled skin.

Kay let go of her arm and stepped back as if

she didn't want to be near Alia any longer than necessary. Neither looked at the other. Instead, they both looked at the Divin.

He was behind a wall of air. The Eldress and two healers were weaving the end of the spell that bound him, the effort of it making them grimace. The Divin stared out at Alia. The cuts on his cheeks were scarlet. His lips twitched with fury. Alia met the Divin's stare. She made herself stand steady, though her knees threatened to buckle.

"Divin Ospar," the Rina said, "you would attack your own?"

"Rina," the Divin responded, his tone full of contempt, "she stands with the enemy, and they are no better than beasts. A farmer kills a dangerous animal before it harms him or his family. Only a witless dolt lets it live."

The room was silent. Though Alia knew she had won, she felt no triumph. The sight of the Divin's true face made her stomach sick.

"And the button?" asked Jen.

"It's mine," answered the Divin. "You warriors continue to let beasts destroy the peace and unity of the provinces. Loose me; I did what had to be done."

"I think the Magus should judge that," said the Rina, expressionless. "Jen, go without stopping to the masters. We need a master and a new divin to come here as soon as they can. Divin Ospar must go to trial."

Grim satisfaction filled Alia. The master would take the Divin, as well as Rhys and Kyrra, to the Magus for the trial. The Divin's evil would be held up for all to see. He had failed.

The small room filled with noise and activity. The healers and the keentens decided to take the Divin to the Sacred House, where the apprentices could help guard him. They began moving him out into the hallway. Mari stayed to speak with Rhys and Kyrra, who seemed more themselves. Alia leaned wearily against the sturdy stone wall. She could feel Kay beside her, just a few paces away. She turned her head, though it seemed so heavy, toward Kay.

"My thanks for speaking up for me," she said.

For many heartbeats, Kay didn't answer. "I saw how you looked at the Rina. You won't become a sister, will you." It was an accusation, not a question.

"I can't," Alia replied quietly.

"I don't understand," Kay said, her words like chips of ice. "But you won't tell me why. You never tell me anything anymore."

"I tried—" Alia started, but Kay interrupted her. "I'm going," Kay said, and she left.

An ache opened up in Alia—deep and dark and bitter. She wanted to drop to her knees and pound on the floor with her fists, but if she moved, the ache might rip wider and wider until she ripped to pieces. She folded her arms and held herself. She was as still as a tree on a windless day. As still as a wood's silence.

Words drifted to her. "They won't execute us," Kyrra said.

"You'll probably have to work as drudges," Mari said as she came over to Alia. "But no executions."

"The Magus won't really punish one of his own, though. Your divin will go free," said Kyrra, sounding tired.

"The punishment for killing with magic is banishment or death," Mari answered. She tucked her hands into her sleeves and seemed to shiver. "I don't know which the Magus will choose, but he'll surely choose one or the other."

"I hope that's so," said Kyrra.

Rhys sat down on a sleeping pallet. "You saved us, Alia," he said as if he couldn't believe it.

"Yes," said Alia. She was surprised to find she could speak.

"Are you all right?" Mari asked Alia.

"Yes," Alia said again.

Mari was quiet a moment. Then she said, "It was a hard thing you did. You have a rare strength."

"My thanks," Alia answered. She tried to smile, but couldn't.

Rhys took up his flute and began to play, his fingers once again nimble and full of grace. Alia listened. The melody rang with the tones of Sophia Wood's ancient words. It pulsed like the golden ridges on her chest.

Alia slipped her hand into her undertunic and felt the trees' mark. At her hand's touch, warmth rippled through it. Bittersweet tears slipped from her eyes. Her old self was gone. But she would not change who she had become.

Fourteen

One morn, less than a moon after Divin Ospar's capture, the apprentices woke to find their binding spells broken and the Divin gone. No one had heard him. No one had seen him. It was as if he had simply disappeared.

The Rins found no tracks. They spoke with the Divin's family. They searched the village and the river, the forests and woods. They sent messages to all the villages nearby. They heard nothing—until word came that a band of men was attacking Beechian warriors and villages with magic. Alia was sure the Divin was one of the band. She hoped the Magus would catch him and the others, and banish them to the farthest deserts of the Borderlands.

Not long after the escape, Master Nest and a tall, thin, soft-spoken divin arrived in Loack. The thin divin was to move into the Divin's Tower and become the leader of the village. Master Nest planned to leave two days later, taking Divin Ospar's family, Rhys, and Kyrra with him. He would take them all across the provinces to the Magus's city. Then, once Divin Ospar and his companions were caught, the Magus would hold a trial. Master Nest supposed that after the trial the Magus would send Rhys and Kyrra to work as drudges until a trade could be arranged for Trantian prisoners in Beech. But Divin Ospar and his companions still ran free, eluding the masters, so Rhys and Kyrra probably would not go home to Beech for many cycles of the seasons.

On the morn before Rhys and Kyrra were to leave, Alia walked to the Prisoner House and went in, shaking a soft covering of snowflakes from her hair. To Jen, who was sitting as guard, she explained why she had come. "Here is the key," said Jen in the careful, cold way the keentens now spoke to her. Since she'd pushed for the truth about the Divin and had chosen not to become a sister, the keentens all treated her like an animal they'd thought was tame but had found was half-wild. They gave her a certain respect but never talked freely near her, never spoke to her at any length or with any warmth.

"My thanks," Alia said, in her own careful, cold way. The warrior women were not what she had thought, either.

She took the key and went down the hallway.

As she opened the cell door, Kyrra smiled. "Well met, Alia."

Alia returned the smile. "Well met, Kyrra, Rhys," she said.

Though Alia had thought that this leavetaking would be quick and simple, now that she stood before Rhys and Kyrra, she didn't know what to say. No one spoke. Kyrra's smile faded. Her fingers plucked at the pouch around her neck. Rhys studied his flute. Alia searched for the right words.

Abruptly, Kyrra said, "If I ever return to Beech, I'll try to find out where your brothers fell. Perhaps a marker could be put on the field."

The offer startled Alia. It took her a moment to find her voice. "My thanks," she said.

Kyrra nodded and bit her bottom lip.

Then, to Alia's surprise, Rhys reached out and took her hand. He bent over and kissed it, his lips just grazing her skin. Shivers flooded up her arm and then washed down her spine. She pulled her hand away too quickly, but he didn't seem to notice.

"My thanks for all you've done," Rhys said, staring at her with his brilliant yellow eyes. "Maybe someday we'll see you again."

Despite the strange shivers, Alia had to smile. The way Rhys spoke almost made her believe him. "Maybe," she answered. "Be well."

Alia turned then and left Rhys and Kyrra for the last time. As she went down the cold, narrow hallway, sadness filled her. She would miss these enemies.

Outside the prison, Alia almost walked into Mari, who was coming up the path. Mari asked, "Are you all right? You look upset."

"I said my farewells to Rhys and Kyrra," Alia said. Mari tilted her head as she listened, as if she could hear not only Alia's words but all the unsayable things underneath them as well.

After a moment Mari said, "No war lasts forever. And I'll hear of them through the Healer Route. You'll know what becomes of them."

"I hope so," Alia answered. There was a little silence. "I should get back. Mam needs me to help with the baby."

"I should go in. I finally have a pair of boots to give to Rhys, and I need to say my farewells." Mari squeezed her arm.

Alia took the back paths toward her farm so she wouldn't see anyone. Since the eve when Divin Ospar's evil had been revealed, everyone—the Smith when she came to the Smithy with Papa, the Speare boys and Tana and Marcus as she walked through the village, even her own brothers and her sister, Sarian, who had come for a visit—treated her strangely. Not that she cared. They could all think what they liked. But she was tired of watching them stare at her as if she were half vengeful spirit, half Old Tales hero.

She took a winding path, one rarely used because it meandered and twisted through fields and forests. She thought she would have it all to herself, but as she came out of a small forest, she heard two sets of snow walkers behind her. The steps were fast, but unusually quiet. She stopped and turned.

Kay burst from the forest with Imorelle at her heels. Kay seemed to misstep at the sight of Alia. Then she ran as fast and as sure as before. She jerked her head in a reluctant greeting. Imorelle gave Alia a shallow nod, as if Alia were beneath her notice. The familiar bitter ache rose in Alia, but she just nodded as she would do at any strangers or distant acquaintances. The girls swerved far around her and ran by.

Alia walked on, trying to push down the bitter ache. Kay still saw things as before. The keentens, if flawed, were still strong and heroic; the life of a warrior woman was still the only true life to strive for; and a girl, a friend, who would refuse to join the sisterhood could not be understood or forgiven. So it shouldn't matter that Imorelle ran with Kay. Or that Kay and Imorelle looked down on her. Or that Alia often walked alone. Because she didn't want to go back to seeing as Kay saw, to being who she once had been.

The bitter ache, though, always rose in her when she and Kay met, and it was always hard to push down.

After the other girls left her sight, Alia veered off on a side path and ran up the last hill before her farm. As she reached the top, she looked out, as she always did now, toward Raven Wood. It was all bright golds and oranges, a glittering blanket on a field of bright white.

Forgetting Kay and Imorelle, she grinned at the wood. Within it were strangenesses and secrets she would learn soon enough. She had shown her leafprint to Mam and Papa and told them that she wished to learn to speak with trees rather than to enter the Keenten House. They had been surprised, but Mam had given Alia a smile and said, "You always would go to any length to avoid house chores, Alia Cateson."

Papa had chewed on his pipe for a long moment. "You're sure you won't enter the Keenten House?" he had asked, gruffly, unable to keep the disappointment from his voice.

She had hesitated, but then had answered him. "I'm sure." His dissatisfied frown had made her sad but had not changed her mind.

Unlike Papa, the Eldress had been pleased by Alia's choice. She'd stared long and hard at her, then had laughed a bit. She'd said that since the village had no other speaker, Alia would apprentice with her in the spring. She'd teach her all she knew of speakers and would find a speaker through the Healer Route who could advise them both. After that, Alia went near Raven and Sophia Woods as often as she could. She had found places, too, where she could hear the woods' songs even if she was standing at a distance from them. For instance, at the door of the Speaker's Shack—which she was helping to repair and clean so it could be a Speaker's House *her* Speaker's House—and near the river's edge and at the hill's top where she now stood.

Alia closed her eyes. She listened, not just with her ears but with her hair and face and skin. Nothing came to her at first. Then, slowly, faintly, singing drifted up and around her, the melody as changeable as the wind. Her leafprint warmed. Heat tingled and sparkled through it.

She threw back her head, and out of her mouth came a wordless song of her own, her voice strong and clear. The trees sang back, louder than before. Alia's song rose and mingled with theirs, the two twisting together until she didn't know which voice was hers and which was theirs.

Words grew from the melody. Alia's tongue caressed them, for they spoke of spring, of sunlight soaking leaves, of roots reaching into warming earth. And then a harmony threaded through the song. *"Alia, ir Allyniar,"* the harmony chanted: "Alia, our Speaker."

The chant sank through Alia, into her bones. It made her voice ring out. She would still ache and she would often be alone, but she was the Allyniar. She was the Speaker.